Moving slowly and gracefully, Darcy swayed to the music.

Her hips rolling, Darcy's arms traced patterns in the air. The exotic music, the sparkle of sequins and shimmer of silk—even the faint incense scent of the air around him—worked a spell on Mike. He felt as if he'd plummeted through a trapdoor from his everyday life to this erotic new world.

Darcy twirled a veil around her, hiding behind it, then revealing the curve of her hip, the smooth paleness of her bare back, the gentle roundness of her belly, the swell of cleavage above the sequined bra top.

Mike's heart pounded and he had trouble breathing, but he made no attempt to turn away.

Dear Reader,

Three and a half years ago I took a belly dancing class. I was looking for some form of exercise that would be fun. The class was fun, all right. So fun I've been dancing ever since.

Though the characters in this book have no connection to the women I've met through my dancing classes, it was a lot of fun to write a story that combines my love of dancing, family and romance.

Life is full of little miracles, and organ transplant is certainly one of those. If you'd like to know more about organ and tissue donation, visit www.organdonor.gov.

I hope you'll enjoy Darcy and Mike's story. I always enjoy hearing from my readers. You can e-mail me at Cindi@CindiMyers.com or through my website www.cindimyers.com.

Cindi Myers

DANCE WITH THE DOCTOR

BY
CINDI MYERS

First published in Great Britain 2011
by Mills & Boon, an imprint of Harlequin (UK) Limited,
Eton House, 18-24 Paradise Road, Richmond, Surrey TW9 1SR

© Cynthia Myers 2010

ISBN: 978 0 263 87918 6

23-1111

Harlequin (UK) policy is to use papers that are natural, renewable and
recyclable products and made from wood grown in sustainable forests. The
logging and manufacturing processes conform to the legal environmental
regulations of the country of origin.

Printed and bound in Spain
by Blackprint CPI, Barcelona

Cindi Myers is the author of more than three dozen novels and a member of an amateur belly dancing troupe, the Mountain Kahai Dancers. She thinks writing and dancing have a lot in common, since both require creativity and a certain amount of chutzpa. She writes and dances in the mountains of Colorado, where she lives with her husband and two spoiled dogs.

For Sheila and the Mountain Kahai Dancers—
especially the Thursday night bunch.

CHAPTER ONE

WHAT WAS I thinking? Darcy O'Connor fought down butterflies as she looked out over the dance studio filled with eight preteen girls who'd signed up for the Belly Dancing for Girlz class. The normally tranquil room had been transformed into a scene of chaos. Dressed in everything from blue jeans and T-shirts to ballet leotards, the girls, ranging in age from nine to eleven, took turns preening and posing in the full-length mirrors lining one wall, draping themselves in the various scarves and costumes that hung around the rest of the room, all talking at once.

Darcy had taught dozens, even hundreds, of women to dance in her four years as a belly dance instructor, but she'd never attempted a class just for girls. When she'd come up with the idea, she'd thought of it as a good way to make children part of her life, but now she wondered if she was really ready for this.

"My aunt Candace took a pole dancing class last summer. Is this anything like that?"

"We saw belly dancers at the Renaissance Festival. My dad stuck a dollar in one of the dancer's bras and my mom got mad."

"I want to dance like Shakira. How long will it take you to teach me to do that?"

"Girls, girls!" Darcy held up her hands. "I'll answer your questions as we go along, but right now let's get started. First, let's line up in rows. Everybody stand where you can see yourself in the mirror."

She moved one of the taller girls, Debby, into the back row, and called forward the smallest of her new students, a delicate child with large brown eyes and a mass of dark brown hair. "Sweetie, you come up here on the front row. What's your name, again?"

"Taylor," the girl said eagerly. She grinned up at Darcy.

"Taylor, you stand next to me. Hannah, you come up on my other side." Darcy surveyed the neat double line of girls in the mirror and felt more in control of the situation. "That's better. Now we can start." She pressed the play button on the remote for the stereo and the first notes of a pop number filled the room. "The first thing we're going to learn is to move our hips from side to side, while the upper part of our bodies stays still."

"My brother says I can't learn to shake my hips because I don't have hips yet," one of the girls, Zoe, volunteered.

"You do too have hips," Kira protested. "Everybody has hips."

"Brothers are just that way," Debby said. "Once mine told me—"

"Now let's try making a circle with our hips," Darcy said, recalling the girls' attention.

"What's this move called?" Liz asked.

"Is it okay if my circle is more of an oval?" Taylor asked.

Darcy smiled to herself. Yes, this class was going to be a challenge, but maybe a challenge was exactly what she needed. "All right, girls. See if you can do this next move. I want everyone to be quiet and listen to the music. Think about how the music makes you feel."

The soaring notes of an Egyptian mizmar filled the air, accompanied by a pounding drumbeat. The music vibrated up through the soles of Darcy's bare feet, soothing her like the caress of a friend. She hoped the girls felt it, too. She wanted to pass on to them more than the mere mechanics of movement.

She caught Taylor's eye in the mirror and was rewarded with a smile that made Darcy's heart skip a beat. There was so much joy and innocence in that smile—so like the smile of her son. A smile she ached to see.

She pushed the sad thought away and struck a dramatic pose as the last notes of the song hung in the air, holding still until someone in the back of the class giggled. Then all the girls dissolved into laughter. Darcy joined them, reaching out to pull Hannah and Taylor close. She'd missed the sound of children's laughter since she'd lost Riley two years ago.

"That was fun." Taylor looked up at her, still smiling. "You're really pretty," the girl said. "Did it hurt when they pierced your nose?"

Darcy laughed. "A little."

Taylor wrinkled her own button nose. "I *hate* needles."

The fierceness in the child's voice both surprised and charmed Darcy. She patted Taylor's back. "There will be no needles in this class. I promise."

"Are we going to learn to dance with swords?" Kira pointed to the pair of curved scimitars that hung over the mirrors at the front of the room. Darcy danced with a sword as part of her professional routine sometimes, but the thought of these girls anywhere near those sharp blades made her blanch.

"You're going to learn a special routine," she said. "We'll spend the next eight weeks learning it and you'll perform it for your parents and friends at my student show in April."

"Will we get to wear costumes?"

"Real belly dancing costumes?"

"I want a pink costume!"

"Can we have bells on them and everything?"

So much for thinking she was in control, Darcy thought, as the girls crowded around her. But she no longer felt nervous or panicky among them. She clapped her hands. "We'll talk about costumes more next week. For now, let's dance some more."

For the rest of the class they played games where

Darcy showed a move and each girl did her best to imitate it. The last five minutes they simply danced. She encouraged the girls to be as silly and uninhibited as they liked, and their excited comments echoed off the walls of the small studio until Darcy's ears rang.

By the end of the hour, everyone was tired but happy, including Darcy. She'd taken an important step today toward putting her life back together. These girls didn't make her miss her son less, but they made her heart less empty.

The girls gathered around the door of the studio to greet arriving parents. Hannah's mother, Darcy's friend Jane, was one of the first to arrive. "How did it go?" she asked.

"It went great, Mom." Hannah held up her cell phone. "I was just texting Kelly all about it. She's going to be so sorry she chose soccer over this." She moved past them out the door, furiously thumbing away.

Jane turned to Darcy. "Well? What do you think?"

"It *was* a blast," Darcy said. "I was worried at first because the girls seemed so scattered, but they really got into it after a bit."

"I'm glad. This was a big step for you." Jane squeezed her hand.

"It was time." For months after Riley's death even the sight of a child on television was enough to cause a flood of tears.

Jane lingered, her eyes fixed on Darcy. "Is something wrong?" Darcy asked.

Jane shook her head. "No. I was just wondering—would you like to go out this weekend?" she asked.

"Go out where?"

"I don't know," Jane said, with studied casualness. "Maybe out to dinner. There's a new steak place over in Kittredge I hear is nice."

"You want to take me out for steak?" Darcy asked.

Jane fidgeted. "Eric has this friend…"

Ah. "No fix-ups." Darcy shook her head.

"He's a really nice guy," Jane persisted. "His name is Mitch and he—"

Darcy didn't cover her ears, though she wanted to. Instead, she put one hand on Jane's arm. "I appreciate the thought, but I'm not interested."

Jane's brown eyes filled with sadness, and her smile vanished. "Okay," she said. "But let me know when you're ready."

That would be never, but Darcy didn't try to explain. Some people, like Jane, who'd been married to Eric for twenty years, were made for happily-ever-after relationships. Others, like Darcy, who came from a family with so many exes and halves and second, third and fourth marriages that they'd have to hire an arena if they ever held a reunion, weren't the long-term-relationship type. Darcy had tried to buck the odds when she'd married Riley's father, Pete, but as much as she'd loved him, things couldn't have turned out worse. She wasn't going to take any more chances.

"Excuse me. Ms. O'Connor?"

Both women turned at the sound of the deep, masculine voice. A broad-shouldered man with dark, curly hair, dressed in an expensive overcoat, greeted them. If Darcy had been asked to use one word to describe the man, she would have chosen "imposing." He had the demeanor of a man used to being in authority.

"I'm Darcy O'Connor," she said, drawing herself up to her full five feet four inches and looking him in the eye, though she had to tilt her head slightly to do so.

Jane squeezed Darcy's arm and waved goodbye, at the same time giving the stranger an appreciative once-over.

"I'm Dr. Mike Carter. Taylor's father."

Darcy saw the resemblance now, in the thick dark curls and brown eyes. Those eyes appeared troubled. She didn't ordinarily have much sympathy for doctors. Her dealings with the medical profession since Riley's death had been mostly unpleasant.

"Hey, Daddy." Taylor joined them, swinging on her father's arm. Dr. Carter looked down at his daughter and smiled, his face so transformed that Darcy caught her breath.

"Hey, sweetheart," he said. "How are you feeling?"

"Great. The class was awesome."

"Are you sure you're okay? You seem flushed."

"Dad!" Taylor's voice rose. "I'm fine."

"Is something wrong?" Darcy asked. Taylor's cheeks were a bit pink, but that was normal after an hour of dancing—wasn't it?

Dr. Carter's gaze remained on his daughter, who was giving him what Darcy could only describe as a warning look. Finally, he said, "Taylor's fine. She's fine now."

Now? "Is there something I need to know?" Darcy asked. Had this man sent his daughter to class sick, possibly exposing a room full of children—not to mention herself?

He shook his head. "I just don't want Taylor to overdo it. Her mother assured me belly dancing wouldn't be too strenuous, though how she'd know that, I have no idea."

Darcy had a vague recollection of a telephone conversation with an enthusiastic woman. "Your wife is the one who signed Taylor up for the class," she said.

"Ex-wife, actually. We're divorced."

Oops.

"I have custody of Taylor, but Melissa sees her as much as possible," he continued. "Her work takes her out of the country quite often."

"My mom's a flight attendant," Taylor offered.

"I'm the one who'll usually be picking up Taylor from class, so I wanted to introduce myself." He looked around her open-concept studio. Wood floors, white walls and windows on three sides. Framed photos of dancers between the windows. Merely stepping into this space was enough to relax Darcy. This was her hard-won sanctuary where grief and fear were absolutely not allowed. She wondered what the doctor, with his expensive coat and patrician air, thought of the humble space. She wouldn't call his expression disapproving, but he was a difficult man to read.

"Do you have children?" he asked.

She stiffened. An innocent enough question, but his tone bothered her—almost as if he was grilling her. *I had a son,* she might have answered. But that was none of his business. "No," she said.

"Do you have experience working with children?"

"Not especially. But I've taught dance full-time for four years and I've danced professionally longer than that." It annoyed her to have to defend herself to this man. She didn't blame him for wanting to know more about the adult who'd be teaching his daughter, but his tone was accusational, as if he suspected her of something.

"Do you have any first-aid training?" he asked. "Do you know CPR?"

Having been the mother of an active boy had taught her plenty of first aid, and she had, in fact, taken a CPR course three years ago. But why did Dr. Carter want to know about that? "Is there a point to all these questions?" she asked.

"I'm concerned for my daughter's safety, that's all."

"I assure you Taylor is perfectly safe here." Did he really think belly dancing was dangerous?

"Dad!" Taylor's tone was anguished. "You're embarrassing me."

His face flushed, and he gave Darcy a look that might have passed for apologetic. "I've tried to tell Taylor it's a father's job to embarrass his child, but she doesn't agree." He took out his wallet and handed her a card. "If you should need to get in touch with me."

She took it. *Michael Carter, M.D. Pediatric Specialist.* He wasn't just any doctor—he was a children's doctor. Was he so cautious with Taylor because he spent his days seeing everything that could go wrong with children? "Thanks," she said, and started to add the card to the pile of papers on the table just inside the door.

"Wait a minute." He stopped her. "Just in case." He took the card back and scribbled on it. "My cell number." He returned it to her. "Nice meeting you," he said, and took Taylor's hand.

"Goodbye, Darcy," Taylor called. "See you next week."

"Goodbye, Taylor. Dr. Carter." When they were gone, Darcy studied his business card again. Had Taylor's father been coming on to her? Why else would he give her his number? After all, it wasn't as if Taylor wouldn't know her father's phone number.

Still puzzling over the doctor's strange behavior, she pulled a coat on over her costume and left the studio, which had once been a detached garage. Though the sun was shining in a Colorado blue sky, the forecast called for more snow by nightfall. She made a mental note to check that the snowblower had plenty of gas.

She walked out to the end of the driveway and collected her mail from the box, then climbed back up to the house. Painted in two shades of green, with a stone patio across the front, it had started life as a weekend getaway for some well-to-do Denverite. In the days before air-conditioning, city folks fled in the summer heat to rustic mountain cabins like this one in Woodbine.

Now they built second homes in Vail and Aspen, leaving the old cabins for people like Darcy to renovate and call home.

She pushed open the front door and shed her coat, pausing, as always, in front of the shelf tucked into an alcove by the door. A swath of bright green Indian silk covered the shelf, on which sat a statue of the Hindu goddess Kali. Cradled in the goddess's many arms was a framed photo of a handsome man with bright red hair and a goatee, and a sandy-haired boy of six, who smiled out of the photo with all the joy and innocence of an angel.

Darcy kissed her finger, then touched the boy's face, her heart tightening as always. The raw grief of missing these two—her husband and son—had lessened in the time since they'd both died in a car accident, but she still felt their absence keenly.

With one last look at the photo, she moved into the living room to sit on the sofa and sort the mail: junk, bill, magazine, junk, junk, bill, ju— She froze in the act of tossing the last letter onto the junk pile. She read the return address on the meter-stamped envelope: Colorado Donor Alliance, Denver.

She stared at it a long time, her insides liquid. Nightmare images filled her head—harsh hospital lighting, beeping monitors, the concern of a woman explaining about organ donation, a pile of paperwork… Darcy struggled to push the ugly memories away. Why were these people contacting her now, after two years?

"They probably just want a donation," she muttered as she tore open the envelope with shaking hands.

Dear Mrs. O'Connor,

Your decision to give the ultimate gift of life by donating your son's, Riley's, organs, has saved the lives of several children. I hope you will take comfort in knowing that some small part of Riley lives on.

Your information and information about organ recipients is always kept in strictest confidence unless both parties give their permission for it to be released. Though some donor families wish to remain forever anonymous, others find closure in meeting the recipients of their gift.

We have recently been contacted by the family of the child who received your son's heart. They would like to meet you, to personally thank you and to allow you to see the results of your decision.

We will be happy to facilitate such a meeting, if you so desire. If you prefer to maintain your anonymity, we will respect that also.

Sincerely,

Mavis Shehadi

Donor Coordinator

Darcy sank back on the sofa and stared, not at the letter in her hand, but at the framed eight-by-ten photo on the wall opposite. Riley, dressed in his green-and-yellow Little League uniform, a bat posed on one shoulder, his hat sitting at a jaunty angle over his blond curls, was frozen in a moment of six-year-old bravado. This was the image of a child who had never known prolonged pain or a moment's real unhappiness.

Darcy had been assured he'd died without suffering. A head injury had damaged his brain, but his other organs had functioned long enough that they could be given to others. The Donor Alliance counselor had assured her that donating Riley's heart, kidneys and liver might spare some other mother the agony Darcy had endured. Overwhelmed by grief and guilt, Darcy had signed the papers, numb to anything but the pain of losing her son. She was convinced she should have done more to save him. Saving his organs for others had seemed such a small thing at the time.

Only later, as some of the blackness receded, had she wondered about those children and their families. But she quickly decided she didn't want to know.

The idea that part of Riley lived on somewhere was comforting in the abstract, but she was afraid hearing about the lives of those children would hurt too much. They got to live…. No amount of heartfelt thanks from other parents could ever make up for the fact that they had their children and she'd lost hers forever.

She'd received a couple of moving letters from grateful parents, their identities carefully blacked out. She'd put them away with other mementos that were too painful to look at—the funeral program, Riley's last report card, his baseball cap.

So she'd never contacted the donor registry and hadn't considered the possibility that they might contact her after all this time.

She reread the letter and waited for the familiar pain to overwhelm her. The guilt was still there, and the ache of longing, but the resentment had faded. That Riley had been taken from her was tremendously unfair, but she would never wish the loss she'd endured on another.

And to think that Riley's heart lived on filled her with a flood of good memories. She had called Riley her sweetheart. When he did something kind for someone, she told him he had a good heart. Before he was born, she had listened to the beating of his heart in her doctor's office and begun to know and love him as someone precious who was part of her, yet his own person.

Did Riley's heart, beating in this other child, sound the same? Would Darcy recognize its rhythm?

What would she do if she *did* recognize something of Riley in this other child? The idea stopped her short.

If she met this child, she wouldn't be anything like Riley, Darcy reassured herself. She had a vague recollection of the donor coordinator telling her Riley's heart was going to a girl. And she would belong to other parents.

Grief was a kind of insanity she only recently felt she'd emerged from. Would meeting this child plunge her back into that darkness, making the loss of Riley fresh again?

She shook her head, and replaced the letter in the envelope. That wasn't a risk she was willing to take. She'd write to the Donor Alliance and refuse. Maybe one day she'd be strong enough to meet one of the transplant children, but she wasn't there yet.

"What did you think of Darcy, Dad?"

Mike glanced in the rearview mirror at his daughter. Taylor leaned forward in the backseat of the car, straining against the seat belt. Only recently had she been able to abandon the booster seat that had been a source of shame for her. Her health problems had left her undersized for her age. Strangers often mistook her for a much younger child.

"Isn't she awesome?"

Awesome was Taylor's word of the moment, used to describe everything from her favorite song on the radio to the macaroni and cheese they'd had for dinner last night. And apparently her new dance teacher. "Ms. O'Connor seems very nice," he said. Though not what he'd expected. "Belly dancer" conjured an image in his mind of someone dark and exotic; Darcy O'Connor was blond and blue-eyed with the kind of curves that would make any man take a second look. Even as concerned as he was for Taylor, Mike had had a hard time not staring.

"She's so beautiful." Taylor ran both hands through her dark curls. "I wish I had hair like hers."

The idea of Taylor with blond curls like Darcy O'Connor almost made Mike smile. "Your hair is beautiful just the way it is," he said.

"You only say that because you're my dad."

Mike felt a pang of regret. Not so long ago his compliments had meant the most simply because he was her dad. Now, apparently, they didn't count for as much.

"I really like the other girls, too," Taylor said. "A couple of them I recognized from school."

"Are any of your friends in it?" he asked. Taylor didn't talk much about her classmates. This hadn't worried Mike before. Yes, all her hospitalizations had put her behind some of her classmates academically. Maybe that had hindered her socially, as well.

"Keisha and Monica are the only girls I really hang out with much at school," Taylor said. "And neither of them is in the class. I think dancing might help me make more friends."

The note of wistfulness in her voice tugged at his heart, and he felt the tightness in his chest from the old anger he could never completely bury. Why had *his* daughter been singled out for such cruelty? Why did *she* have to suffer so much? "I'm sure you'll make friends," he said.

"I think so." She sat back in the seat. "It's kind of

special, you know? Being part of the dance group, I mean. I'll bet a lot of girls wish they could be in it."

Mike forced himself to loosen his grip on the steering wheel and reminded himself that in spite of everything, Taylor had been very lucky. She was alive, and likely to live a long, happy life, if she was careful. He turned onto Sycamore Street. "Did you remember to take your medicine?" he asked.

"Yes. I took it before class."

"Good." She'd been so excited about the dance class he'd been afraid she'd forget. It needed to be taken on a strict schedule. "I want you to be honest with me—you didn't overdo it today, did you? The class wasn't too strenuous?"

"No. It was fun. Darcy's a really good dancer."

Darcy again. Taylor was clearly captivated by her attractive teacher. "I imagine she's been practicing for quite a few years." Though how long could that be, really? Maybe her petite size made her look young for her age, but she hadn't seemed a day over twenty-five to Mike. At thirty-six, he felt positively ancient next to her.

"If I start now, I could be that good by the time I graduate high school."

"I thought you wanted to be a doctor." He tried to keep his voice neutral.

"I do. But I could belly dance on the side. As a hobby."

A belly dancing doctor. "That would certainly give your patients something to talk about."

"Dad, please!" Taylor's voice drifted toward an unpleasant whine. "You're always telling people how important it is to exercise. Dancing will be good for me."

It probably would. And she was bored with spending so much time at his office after school, where he worried she might come down with an opportunistic infection despite all his precautions. But he hadn't found a sitter he trusted and he couldn't leave Taylor at home alone.

Even two years out from her transplant surgery, she was still so vulnerable. How could he trust her with a woman he barely knew? "Like it or not, you're always going to be more vulnerable than other people to illness," he said. "What if something happened while you were in dance class? What if you have a reaction to one of your medications?"

"Dad, that only happened one time! And it was months ago."

"But what if it happened? I don't know if Darcy is prepared to handle that."

"She would do the same thing they would do at school—she'd call nine-one-one."

Taylor had to go to school, but Mike tried to keep her away from large groups of people otherwise. Maybe he was being overly cautious, or even silly, but he couldn't help himself. The knowledge of everything that could go wrong, and the memory of how close he'd come to losing the most precious person to him, haunted him. "I'd be happier if you'd wait a little longer," he said. The past two years had been a nightmare of hospital rooms and surgeries, antirejection drugs, infections and the constant fear that something as simple as a cold virus could undo all her progress.

"I just want to do something a normal kid would do."

The plaintive words cut through him. Wasn't that all he wanted, too—for his little girl to be happy and healthy, and to live a full, normal life? And she was doing better. She'd started growing, and it had been four months since she'd been sick a single day.

"I know," he said. "And dance class will probably be fine. But if you have any problems at all…"

"I'll have to quit. But I'll be fine, I promise. Thank you, Daddy. I love you."

"I love you too, sweetheart." All that love made making the right decisions for her even harder sometimes.

They pulled up to their townhome and Mike pressed the button to open the garage. He and Melissa had purchased the home shortly after their wedding. When they'd divorced they'd both agreed it would be better for Taylor to remain in the only home she'd ever known, and Melissa had moved into an apartment near the airport, convenient to her work. If not for Taylor, Mike would have moved, too. The house was one more reminder of dreams that hadn't come true. He and Melissa had planned to raise a family in this home.

Taylor was out of the car as soon as Mike released the child locks. "I'm gonna call Mom and tell her about the class," she called over her shoulder as she raced to the door.

Mike hoped Melissa would be able to answer Taylor's call. If she was in the middle of a flight that wasn't possible. Taylor could leave a message, but Melissa wasn't always good about returning her calls right away.

He followed Taylor inside, stopping to hang his coat on the rack in the foyer, opposite the portrait of the three of them as a family. Melissa smiled straight into the camera; a younger Mike focused on the toddler in Melissa's lap. Taylor, in a lacy white dress, had been barely two then. She was laughing up at Mike—the happiest baby in the world.

And he'd been the happiest man, just beginning his practice, starting a family. How naive he'd been.

Taylor's illness had changed all that. Mike didn't know if he'd ever trust happiness again. He'd always be waiting for the other shoe to drop. He'd emerged from more than two years in hell with his daughter safe, for now, but the perfect family was gone. The messiness—both emotional and physical—of dealing with a chronically ill child had ended a marriage already strained by Mike's long hours at work and Melissa's erratic schedule.

The failure to save his marriage still stung. Mike's parents had been married more than forty years now, while his grandparents had lived to celebrate seventy-five years together. His two sisters both enjoyed long marriages. Only Mike had failed.

He didn't blame Melissa. Mike had deserted her when she needed him most. He'd been too focused on Taylor and on keeping his practice going to have much left over for his wife.

He found Taylor in the living room, curled on one end of the sofa, the phone still in her lap. "Did you talk to your mom?" he asked.

"I had to leave a message." Her shoulders drooped.

"I should talk to your mother about setting up a schedule to see you more often," Mike said. As it was, Melissa flew in and out of town, and her daughter's life, with no predictable regularity. Taylor missed her mother, though she seldom said it.

He and Melissa had agreed to family counseling to help Taylor deal with the divorce, but her frequent hospitalizations had interfered with those sessions, and Mike wasn't sure how much good they'd done. Taylor seemed well adjusted to their situation, but how could he be sure?

Right now, Taylor looked as worried as he felt. She was chewing on her lower lip, an unattractive habit he'd tried to discourage. "Honey, is something wrong?"

She glanced at him, then away. "Mom told me something last time I saw her. She didn't tell me not to tell you, but I'm not sure you're going to like it."

"What is it?" What had Melissa done that had Taylor so worried?

"She said she has a boyfriend. His name is Alex and he's a pilot."

"Oh." He shifted in his chair, trying to get comfortable with the idea of his wife—he still thought of her that way sometimes—dating another man. The emotion that rose to the surface wasn't so much jealousy as regret that things hadn't worked out the way they were supposed to.

One of them ought to at least be happy; he wouldn't begrudge Melissa that. "That's good, honey," he said. "Are you okay with it?"

"It would be nice if she had someone, so she wouldn't be alone," Taylor said thoughtfully. "I mean, you and I have each other, except..." The words trailed away.

"Except what?"

"Do you think you'll ever get married again, Dad?"

Was Melissa close to marrying this guy? Was that why she'd mentioned him to Taylor? "I don't plan on getting married again, honey," he said. "Not for a very long time, anyway." Not before Taylor was grown, if then. He'd already proved he was lousy at dividing his attention.

"I wouldn't mind if you did," she said. "I mean, I wouldn't mind having a stepmom, if she was nice."

So that's what this was all about. Mike moved to sit beside his daughter and pulled her close. "I know you miss your mom," he said. "There's not much I can do about that, but I'm not sure a stepmom is the answer. You and I will just have to muddle along like we have been." He kissed the top of her head.

"I'm okay, Dad." She squirmed around to look up at him. "Really. I just thought you might, you know, be lonely sometimes."

Yes, he was lonely sometimes, but he'd survive. "Don't worry about me, sweetheart," he said. Life demanded sacrifices sometimes. Right now his priorities were Taylor and his medical practice, in that order. Any woman in his life would be shortchanged. He wouldn't put himself or anyone else through that hurt again.

CHAPTER TWO

"SISTER, DEAR, if you lived a more normal life, this kind of thing wouldn't happen."

Darcy helped her older brother, Dave, wrestle the snowblower from the snowbank where it had skidded and stopped working. "I do—" *puff* "—have a normal—" *puff* "—life," she said. "At least it's not *abnormal*."

"If you had a normal life you'd store your snowblower in your garage instead of using the space for a dance studio. Then parts wouldn't rust and you wouldn't have to call me to come to the rescue."

"You love playing the big, strong hero and you know it." She folded her arms over her chest and watched him tinker with something on the snowblower. "Can you fix it?"

"What do you mean, can I fix it? Of course I can fix it."

"Can you fix it today? In time to finish my driveway before my evening classes?"

"No, I cannot." He reached in and yanked something loose and held it up. "I'm going to have to order this part. Depending on how hard it is to find or how long it takes to ship from the factory, you may be shoveling for a few weeks."

She groaned. Not that she wasn't capable of shoveling out her driveway, but it took a lot longer than running the snowblower, not to mention she almost always ended up hurting her back. "I don't suppose you'd let me borrow *your* snowblower in the meantime?"

"I'm not even that generous with my girlfriend, much less my sister." He straightened and wiped his hands on his pants. "Maybe you ought to put on one of those belly dancing costumes and see if you can persuade some big, strong guy to shovel for you. Either that, or pray it doesn't snow again between now and whenever the part comes in."

"Or I'll just shovel it myself. And speaking of girlfriends, how is Carrie?" Dave and Carrie Kinkaid had dated on and off for five years. Lately it was definitely more on than off.

"Carrie is fine. She dyed her hair red and it looks great. I told her it was like dating a new woman without all the first-date trauma."

"You're such a romantic. When are you two going to get married?"

"Why should we get married? Things are good between us the way they are."

"You can't just date each other forever."

"Why not? Seems like our family does a lot better at dating than marriage."

Darcy grimaced. Whereas it bothered her that their family had so many failed relationships, Dave seemed to take a perverse pride in their poor track record. "Somebody ought to be the first to break the family curse," she said. "Why not you?"

"You beat me to it," he said. "You were a great wife and an even better mom."

He meant to cheer her up with the compliment, but it only served to remind her of what might have been. "Pete and I didn't have a perfect marriage." Toward the end, especially, they'd had big problems, problems that only added to Darcy's guilt.

"Who does? But you made it work. And I never saw anyone happier than you were with Riley."

She nodded, afraid her voice might break if she tried to say anything. From the time she was a girl she'd wanted to be a mom. She'd loved babysitting and was always ready to help with her younger cousins. When Riley had been born she'd been over the moon. She hadn't meant for him to be an only child, but the time had never been right for another baby, though before the accident she'd decided she and Pete should try for another child soon.

Dave left the snowblower and put his hand on her shoulder. "You should have more kids," he said. "Not to replace Riley, but because you were meant to be a mother."

She shook her head. "I think maybe…I'm the type of person who's better off without that kind of responsibility." How could she bear to love another child, knowing that at any moment she could do the wrong thing—make the wrong choice—and he could be taken away from her?

"That's crazy."

"No crazier than you not wanting to marry the woman you love."

"Right." He took his hand from her shoulder. "Then I guess we're just a family of loony tunes. Come on—find me a shovel and I'll help clear your driveway."

"Now that's the way to be a good brother."

He grinned. "It's just an excuse to hang around until your adult students start to show up in their skimpy costumes."

She swatted his back. "Don't you dare ogle my dancers."

"Why not? Some of them might like it."

"I'm going to tell Carrie you said that."

"She doesn't care if I look. And don't try to pretend you don't like it when men look—otherwise, you wouldn't dress in those costumes."

She sighed. "Okay, I'll admit it. I worked hard for these abs, and I don't mind showing them off. But that is *not* all dancing is about."

"If you say so."

He dodged her next blow and grabbed up the snow shovel. "If you want the driveway done, step out of my way. And be nice to me. I'm the only man in your life right now, so you might want to keep me around."

"Sure. But only for your muscles."

"You know you love me."

"I do love you." Sometimes it was nice to have a little testosterone around the house, even if he was related to her. Men, like children, had a different perspective on life. She hadn't always agreed with Pete's point of view about things, but sometimes he had helped her see a situation in a new light, and that was probably healthy.

But the opportunity to hear the male perspective wasn't a big enough benefit to risk another botched relationship. She might joke with Dave about breaking the family curse, but she believed in that curse. Maybe she and Dave and the rest of her relatives weren't meant for the lifelong monogamy she'd always idealized, in the same way some people didn't have a talent for math or a good sense of direction.

She'd never been much of a gambler, but since the accident all she wanted was to play it safe. If that meant being alone, well, there were worse things in the world. Whoever said it was better to have loved and lost than to never have loved at all didn't know what he was talking about.

THE STUDENTS ARRIVED for their Wednesday afternoon dance class in a rush of cold wind and chaos. Most of them, including Taylor, walked up the hill to Darcy's house from the bus stop, and surged into the studio, wrestling off backpacks, coats and shoes, chattering like a flock of parrots. Darcy stood to one side and watched, letting the energy and vitality of these young people wash over her.

When their conversation had subsided to a low murmur, Darcy stepped to the front of the room and clapped her hands. "Today we're going to start learning the routine you'll perform for your parents and friends in April," she announced. "Everyone in your places so we can get started."

Music up, Darcy led the way through the first few moves of the routine she'd choreographed with the girls in mind. The moves were simple but lovely, challenging enough to keep them entertained and to impress their families, and a foundation they could build on if they decided to continue studying belly dance. She watched in the mirror as they practiced the moves, the girls all smiles. Next to her, Taylor was grinning so broadly Darcy wondered it didn't hurt.

"What kind of costumes will we wear in the show?" Debby asked from the back row as they practiced moving their hips in a figure-eight pattern.

"You can wear a skirt or pants and a top, and a hip scarf with coins," Darcy said. "Something similar to what the adult dancers wear."

"My mom said she'd make me a pink costume," Jane's daughter Hannah said.

"Where do you get a costume?" Zoe asked. "Can you just buy one?"

"You probably already have some skirts and tops at home you can use," Darcy said. "Your moms—or dads—can decorate them with sequins or beads." She smiled at the thought of Dr. Mike sewing sequins on a tiny top.

"What color costume do you want, Taylor?" Hannah asked.

Taylor shrugged.

"Well, what's your favorite color?" Hannah persisted.

"Purple."

While the others discussed the merits of skirts versus pants and sequins versus beads, Darcy was aware that Taylor had become very quiet. Her smile had vanished, and she seemed almost to have shrunk into herself. "Is something wrong, sweetie?" Darcy asked.

Taylor shook her head, not meeting Darcy's eyes.

Clearly something was wrong. "Are you worried about your costume?" she asked. Maybe Taylor thought Mike would object to her wearing one. Or that a dad wasn't qualified to help her put one together. Darcy bent low, and whispered, "I'll help you find the right thing to wear. Don't worry."

Taylor nodded, though she didn't look much happier.

"Darcy, will you dance for us, please?" Liz asked.

"Yes, please! We want to see you dance!"

The other girls added their pleas.

Darcy had planned to finish out class with a version of Simon Says using dance moves, but it would be fun to perform for the girls. She could show them some of the things they'd be able to do if they continued to study and practice. "All right," she said. "Everyone sit on the floor at the back of the studio and I'll dance for you."

"With the sword," Kira said.

"Not with the sword," Darcy said. "With a veil." She plucked a large gauzy blue silk one, spangled with sequins, from a shelf near the door. "Now just give me a minute to find the right music." She felt a familiar tickle of excitement low in her stomach. Nothing like performing for an appreciative audience to make a dancer want to do her best.

ON WEDNESDAYS, Mike closed his office early. Most of the time he and Taylor did something special together. They went to the movies or out for pizza. Now that she was in dance class, he missed her more than he'd imagined. The office seemed emptier without her chatter, and he felt at loose ends, wondering what she was up to, and if she was all right. In a few more weeks he'd adjust to the change in routine, just as he'd adjusted to her return to school after her last hospitalization and her overnight visits with her mother. But for now her absence left him unsettled.

Nicole stopped in the doorway of his office. "Your last patient is ready," the nurse said.

Grateful for the distraction of work, Mike headed for Exam Room One, where nine-year-old Brent Jankowski waited, along with his mom, Sarah, and three younger sisters. "What's up with you today, Brent?" Mike asked, glancing at the boy's chart.

"I have a cold." Brent sniffed.

"I hate to bother you with such a silly thing." Sarah looked up from tying her youngest's—Emily's—shoe. "But you did tell us we should come in for any sign of illness at all."

"Yes, it's smart to be careful." Mike put his stethoscope to Brent's chest and listened. There, under the normal lub-dub of the heart was a soft, sighing sound—a leaky heart valve. It was just the sort of defect that could lead to bigger problems down the road. Even something as routine as a common cold could turn more serious for Brent, as it had for Taylor. Fortunately, advanced diagnostics had caught the problem earlier and new treatment protocols promised a more favorable outcome than Taylor's.

Mike moved the stethoscope to listen to the boy's lungs, then checked his ears and throat. "There's bronchitis setting in," he said. "I'm going to prescribe a heavy-duty decongestant. We'll try to avoid antibiotics for now, but if he starts running a fever above a hundred, call me right away."

"All right. Thanks."

As he typed the prescription into the computer, he marveled at Sarah Jankowski's calm. He started imagining worst-case scenarios every time Taylor sneezed. Maybe Sarah's blasé attitude came from having four children instead of only one.

He'd wanted more children, despite his long work hours, but Melissa had been as reluctant as he was to take time off from her job and felt one child was plenty.

He saw the Jankowskis to the front desk, then glanced at the clock. He still had a few minutes before it was time to pick Taylor up from her class, but it wouldn't hurt if he arrived early.

When he pulled into the driveway and switched off the car he could hear music coming from the garage-turned-studio. He could make out drums and some kind of high-pitched instrument, maybe a flute. Smiling to himself, he slid out of the car. He'd just peek in, try to catch a glimpse of Taylor dancing without her realizing he was watching.

Snow crunched under his feet as he followed the path to the studio. He slipped through the foyer to a second door behind which the music throbbed. He eased it open and peeked inside.

But instead of watching Taylor and the other students, he found himself staring at Darcy, her back to the door, performing for a wide-eyed group of girls.

Moving slowly and gracefully, Darcy swayed in rhythm to the music, hips rolling, arms tracing patterns in the air. The exotic music, the sparkle of sequins and shimmer or silk, even the faint incense in the air, worked a spell on Mike. He felt as if he'd plummeted through a trapdoor from his everyday life to this erotic new world. Darcy twirled a veil around her, hiding, then revealing the curve of her hip, the smooth paleness of her bare back, the gentle roundness of her belly, the swell of cleavage above the sequined bra top. Mike's heart pounded and he had trouble breathing, but he made no attempt to turn away.

His life was so devoid of the feminine. The sexual. He wasn't the type of man who looked at magazine centerfolds or visited topless bars. He hadn't dated since his divorce, his life consumed by work and caring for his daughter. The sexual side of him was there, but it wasn't convenient or practical to think about it. Watching Darcy, he was thinking about it now.

The tempo of the song increased. Drums pounded and flutes trilled. Darcy whirled, hips bouncing, the bells on the blue scarf knotted over low-slung blue velvet pants chiming furiously. Mike stared, mesmerized, as she undulated and shimmied, hips, then stomach, then chest. Trying to regain his composure, he lowered his gaze to the floor, watching her feet, but this was no help; Darcy even had sexy feet, small with high arches and pink-painted toenails.

The music ended abruptly, with a drumroll. Darcy froze, arms over her head, breathing hard. The girls erupted into applause. "That was so awesome!" Taylor gushed. "Dad, wasn't that fantastic?"

All eyes turned toward the door, including Darcy's. Mike felt as guilty as a schoolboy, but tried not to show it. He stepped into the room. "That was…very impressive," he said.

Taylor ran to greet him, swinging on his hand. "Wouldn't it be great if I could do that?"

The thought of his little girl shimmying and undulating to exotic music, dressed in a skimpy costume, made Mike queasy. Of course Taylor had to grow up someday, but she was only ten….

His thoughts must have shown on his face, because Darcy laughed. "Go easy on your father, Taylor. Dads have a hard time thinking of their daughters as all grown-up."

She couldn't know how especially hard it was for him, after having once faced the very real possibility that Taylor would never grow up at all.

He turned to her. "I hope you don't mind that I watched your dance. I got here early and heard the music and thought I might catch a glimpse of Taylor."

"Of course I don't mind," she said. "I'm used to performing for an audience."

"Do you do shows often? I mean, for the public?"

"I dance at a restaurant in Denver—Arabica— most Friday evenings. You're welcome to come watch anytime." Her eyes sparkled. Was she flirting with him?

He smiled. "I might do that sometime." Not that he would, but there was no harm in pretending. It felt good to interact with a woman who wasn't the mother of one of his patients or Taylor's teacher.

Other parents began arriving and Darcy turned to greet them. There was a flurry of donning coats and finding backpacks, then calls of "Goodbye!" and "See you next week!"

Then Taylor was at Mike's side, tugging at his hand. "Dad!"

"What is it, hon?"

"I forgot to take my meds before class." Worry made a deep V between her brows. "I thought about it on the bus, but then when we got here I was so excited…"

"It's okay." He patted her shoulder, as much to reassure himself as her. True, the medications were supposed to be taken at regular intervals, but there was nothing to be done about it right now. Later, at home, he'd emphasize to Taylor again the importance of keeping on schedule. Maybe he could set up a

reminder on her phone. "You can take them now."
He turned to Darcy, who was closing the studio door
behind the rest of the parents. "Could Taylor have a
glass of water?" he asked. "She needs to take some
pills."

"Pills?" Darcy looked at Taylor, who blushed and
stared at the floor. "Of course. Come up to the house
with me."

DARCY LED the way up the path to her house, hur-
rying her steps, aware of the anxiety radiating from
the girl at her heels. Taylor looked so ordinary and
healthy—why would she need to take pills?

"One glass of water, coming up," she said once
they were in the kitchen. She got a glass from the
cabinet, while Taylor opened her backpack on the
kitchen table. Mike stood just inside the door, hands
shoved in his trouser pockets, studying the photograph in Kali's arms.

"The boy looks like you," he said.

Darcy turned from the sink, glass of water in her
hand. "Excuse me?"

Mike nodded at the picture of Pete and Riley. "The
boy looks like you. He has your eyes."

Darcy handed the glass to Taylor. "That's my son.
Riley. And his father, Pete. They were both killed in
a car wreck two years ago." There was no easy way
to reveal this tragedy—better to say it straight out.

"Oh." He was clearly shocked. "I'm very sorry."

"Thank you." The kindness in his eyes touched the tender spot inside her where the pain was still raw. She looked away, focusing on Taylor. "What kind of pills do you have to take?"

Taylor pulled a pill case from her backpack—the plastic kind with multiple compartments. "This is Gengraf and that one is CellCept. This is prednisone, that's quinine and this one is Zantac." She rattled off the names of the drugs as if she was reciting a list of favorite music groups or the names of relatives.

"You take all these every day?" Darcy asked, stunned.

"Most of them three times a day—the prednisone and quinine only once. I was taking some drugs five times. Dad says as I get older, I should be able to get down to taking meds only twice a day, and some of them I should be able to stop altogether."

Darcy swallowed a calcium pill at breakfast and the occasional pain reliever for cramps. She couldn't imagine a life of ingesting what amounted to the stock of a small pharmacy every day. Mike was frowning at the array of pills laid out in front of his daughter. "Why does she need all this?" Darcy asked.

"The Gengraf and CellCept are antirejection drugs," Taylor said, ignoring that the question hadn't been directed at her. "But they give me leg cramps, so that's why I take the quinine. The prednisone upsets my stomach, so I take the Zantac for that. The prednisone also used to make my face swell, but not so much anymore."

She spoke matter-of-factly, as if this was all normal. Darcy continued to stare at Mike. He raised his eyes from the line of pills and met Darcy's gaze. She was struck again by the sadness there. "Two years ago, Taylor had a heart transplant," he said. "She's doing great now, but the medications are an important part of her treatment."

"A heart transplant." Darcy lowered herself into a chair at the kitchen table, suddenly too weak to stand. She swallowed, trying to bring moisture into her too-dry mouth. In a voice that to her ears didn't sound like her own, she said, "So—she received a heart from a donor?"

"A boy." Taylor popped the last pill into her mouth and drained the last of the water. "We don't know his name, but he was six years old." She set the empty glass on the table. "Thank you for the water."

Darcy closed her eyes, fighting dizziness. That was a mistake. As soon as her eyes closed, scenes from her last moments with Riley flashed in front of her. Riley lying still and small in the hospital bed, the only sound the whir and beep of the machines that kept his heart beating. The Donor Alliance co-ordinator with a sheaf of paperwork, explaining the donation procedure. *The doctors think they have a match for your son's heart. A little girl.*

"Darcy, are you all right?"

She felt a hand on her shoulder and looked up into Mike's eyes. "Do you feel faint?" he asked. "You're white as a sheet."

Darcy shook her head and studied Taylor, who stood apart, eyes wide. "The boy who donated your heart—you don't know his name?"

Taylor looked at her dad. "I don't think they ever told us."

"No," Mike said. "That information is kept confidential unless both families agree for it to be released."

Darcy stood, a little shakily. "Maybe you'd better sit back down," Mike said. "You still seem very pale."

She shook her head and crossed to the basket beneath the telephone where she kept the mail. She sorted through the stack of bills and flyers and unearthed the cream-colored envelope from the Donor Alliance. "Read that," she said, handing it to Mike.

He pulled out the letter and stared at it. Darcy kept her eyes on the floral pattern of the tiles on her kitchen floor. She focused on breathing slowly through her nose, inhaling the aroma of basil and oregano from last night's spaghetti dinner, and the faint strawberry-shampoo scent of Taylor. Taylor, who was standing here today because a boy had died, a boy like Riley.

Mike folded the letter and replaced it in the envelope. "When did your son die?" he asked.

"January twenty-first, two thousand and eight."

"The same day as my transplant," Taylor said. She took a step closer to Darcy. "Do you think I have his heart?"

"Except that I never contacted the donor registry," Mike said. "It's possible there were two transplants performed that day."

"Oh." Darcy hadn't thought of that. She was surprised at how disappointed she felt.

"Dad?"

Both adults turned to the girl, who looked as if she'd just been caught cheating on a math test. "I...I wrote a letter to the Donor Alliance."

"You did?" Mike frowned. "When?"

"A few weeks ago. I've been thinking a lot about the boy who gave me his heart and...and I just wanted to know."

"Why didn't you tell me?" Mike said, clearly stricken.

"I didn't want to upset you," Taylor said. "You always said it would be better not to know my donor's identity, that the family deserved their privacy. But I really wanted to know." She bit her lower lip. "I took some stationery from your desk and pretended to be you. I thought if the donor family wrote back and said they wanted to meet me, then I'd tell you and it would be all right."

"You lied, Taylor," Mike said. "That's wrong."

"But I thought it didn't really matter, since the donor family never answered."

"It's not that I didn't want to know about the child who got Riley's heart," Darcy said. "I just…I guess I was afraid. That it might be too hard."

Mike put his hand on her shoulder. She wanted to lean into that comforting weight, to draw strength from him. "I'm sorry this has upset you," he said.

"It's all right." Taylor still looked guilty, and a little scared. "Really, it's fine," Darcy said. "I'll admit it was a shock, but if you do have Riley's heart, I'm glad. Truly, I am."

"We don't know for sure your son was Taylor's donor," Mike said.

"That's true," Darcy said. The transplant had been performed at Denver Children's Hospital. The recipient of Riley's heart could have come from anywhere in the area, even from Wyoming. But the timing couldn't be a coincidence. How likely was it that two heart transplants had been performed that fateful day?

"What did you say your son's name was?" Taylor asked.

"Riley. He was big for his age. Maybe his heart was a little bigger too, and that's why it was a good fit for you." Darcy glanced at Mike. "Could that be right?"

"Yes, it could."

"Do you have a picture of Riley?" Taylor asked.

"Over there." Darcy nodded at the picture of Riley and Pete by the door. "But there's a better one in here." She led the way to the living room, and the portrait of Riley in his baseball uniform. "That was taken a couple of weeks before...before the accident."

"He's cute," Taylor said. "I like his freckles."

"I imagine the two of you could have been friends," Darcy said. When he'd died, Riley had been at the age where he thought of girls as "icky" but maybe by now he'd see them differently. Darcy swallowed hard. No. She couldn't let her thoughts dwell on what might have been. Mike had joined them in the living room. "Why did Taylor need the transplant?" she asked.

His sadness intensified. Had she been out of line to ask him to recall what must have been a terrifying time? But it was too late to take back the question now. "When she was nine she developed cardiomyopathy," he said. "An inflammation of the heart muscle. It's usually caused by some kind of infection, but we're not sure what caused it or where it came from. By the time hers was diagnosed, the heart muscle was damaged beyond repair."

"How horrible."

"I know what you're thinking," he said. "How could a pediatrician have missed such a serious illness in his own daughter? But it's not like the flu or an infected toenail. And Taylor isn't the type to complain."

"I wasn't thinking any such thing," she said. Mike

clearly adored his daughter. But she recognized his guilt—those silent accusations that intimated her son would be okay today if she had only been a better parent.

"There's no danger now," Mike said. "As long as Taylor's careful and remembers to take her medication."

"I was distracted today," Taylor said, blushing. "I won't forget again." She glanced at Darcy. "Dad's always worried I'm going to overdo it, or that I'll catch some infection from someone. He doesn't even like me to go to the mall."

"He wants to protect you," Darcy said. "It's what parents do."

"I think it's 'cause he's a doctor," Taylor said. "He sees sick people all day and reads medical journals full of articles about horrible diseases, then he imagines everything bad that can happen."

That wasn't it, Darcy thought. Mike knew all the bad things that could happen because he'd lived them. Children weren't supposed to have to get new hearts to stay alive, but his had. Who could blame him for fearing the worst after that? "You're lucky to have a father who cares so much."

Mike sent her a look of gratitude and sympathy. How had she ever lumped him with the arrogant and distant physicians she'd encountered? Though in truth, maybe even those doctors weren't so bad, and her impressions were colored by the circumstances.

Still, Mike was different. Losing a child, or almost losing one, left scars only someone who had been through the same thing could understand. "Come on, Taylor, it's time we went home," Mike said. "Back to your life of drudgery and oppression."

Taylor rolled her eyes.

Darcy walked them to the door. Taylor ran ahead to the car, but Mike paused for a moment. "Will you contact the Donor Alliance?" he asked.

"Yes. Just to confirm our suspicions."

"I'm sorry if this has upset you."

She glanced past him, at Taylor climbing into the backseat of the car. She'd been drawn to Taylor from their first meeting. Was it because she recognized something of her son in the child? "I'm glad you were able to find a donor for her, even if it wasn't Riley."

"Thank you." He joined her in watching Taylor. "She's right," he said. "I do worry too much. I can't seem to help it."

"Maybe you'll worry less as she gets older." And stronger. Surely every year past the surgery meant a better prognosis for Taylor. Mike would see his daughter grow up, and all the worry would be worth that joy. At least that's what she imagined she'd feel if their roles were reversed.

CHAPTER THREE

"THIS SITUATION IS very irregular." Mavis Shehadi, Donor Coordinator for the Colorado Donor Alliance, studied the two adults and the child in chairs before her desk. "So you met entirely by coincidence." She shook her head. "I've heard some unusual stories in my time here, but this is one of the more unbelievable ones."

"Are you going to spend the rest of this meeting questioning our motives," Mike said, "or are you going to tell us what we came here to find out?"

Darcy sympathized with Mike's anger. She was also losing patience with Ms. Shehadi. "I don't see that it matters how we came to meet," she said. "Taylor received a heart transplant the same day my son's heart was donated. All we want to know now is whether or not Taylor has Riley's heart."

But Ms. Shehadi wasn't going to let them bypass proper channels any further. "I sent a letter ten days ago alerting you to a request we'd had from the recipient of your son's heart to meet with you," she said. "I didn't find any record in our files that you'd answered."

Darcy shifted on the hard chair. "No, I didn't answer. At the time, I wasn't sure if I was ready to meet the family."

"And you think you're ready now."

"Yes." Her doubts had vanished when she'd heard Taylor's story, putting a face—a real, live girl—to the story of the anonymous child who lived because her son had died. Knowing Taylor didn't make Darcy miss Riley any less, but neither did it make her mourn him more, as she'd originally worried.

"Are you ready because you've established a relationship with Dr. Carter and his daughter and you feel this would further that, or because you're truly ready to know the truth?" Ms. Shehadi's expression remained impassive.

"What are you suggesting?" Mike asked, his body tense, his voice too loud.

What was she suggesting, indeed? That Darcy had designs on Mike and thought this was a way to get closer to him?

"It's my job to ask these questions," Ms. Shehadi said softly. "Meeting someone, especially a child who lives because of the donation of part of someone you loved very much, can have a profound emotional impact on both parties. Usually we require both the donor's and the recipient's family to undergo counseling before we arrange the meeting. In a case like this, where you've skipped those steps, I want to do what I can to make sure there's no emotional fallout."

Emotional fallout. Darcy sat back in her chair. Cold words for the heated turmoil inside her. These past few nights had been full of too many dreams about the last moments of Riley's life. She'd relived all the guilt and regret, but that didn't mean she blamed Taylor or Mike for any of those emotions. And she'd reached a point where not knowing the truth was worse than knowing it.

"Can you just tell us?" she asked. "Did Riley's heart go to Taylor?"

"Yes."

One short syllable, but it meant so much. Darcy turned to Taylor, the image of the girl blurred by tears. She forced herself to smile. She resisted the urge to reach out and touch Taylor, to satisfy the longing to embrace the child who kept something of Riley alive.

"I promise I'll take very good care of Riley's heart," Taylor said solemnly.

That almost undid Darcy. She struggled to retain her composure.

"Dr. Carter, how do you feel about this?" Ms. Shehadi asked. "I'm assuming, since you originally contacted the donor registry, that you're satisfied with this outcome."

Mike's mouth twitched, and he glanced at Taylor, who squirmed in her chair. "I'm fine," he said.

"What about Mrs. Carter? Is there a reason she isn't here today?"

"Taylor's mother and I are divorced," Mike said. "She couldn't be here today because she's in Germany on business."

Did Darcy imagine the slight irritation in his voice? She wondered if he was upset with Ms. Shehadi, or with his absent ex-wife. It struck Darcy as odd that Taylor's mother wasn't here today. In her place, Darcy would have wanted to reassure and support Taylor. But perhaps the ex–Mrs. Carter felt Mike, as custodial parent, was better equipped for that task.

"Would either of you like to take advantage of the counseling sessions we offer?" Ms. Shehadi asked.

"No thank you." The last thing Darcy wanted was to discuss her personal feelings with a stranger.

"That won't be necessary," Mike said.

Ms. Shehadi continued to study them. Maybe she was merely peeved at having been left out of their original meeting. "Do any of you have questions for me?"

"No." Mike and Darcy both spoke at once. Darcy stood, and Mike followed her example. Apparently, he was as anxious to escape the office as she was.

"Thank you for your help," Darcy said, and offered her hand to Ms. Shehadi.

"Yes. Thank you." Mike also shook hands, then he was ushering Darcy and Taylor into the hallway. "I don't think Ms. Shehadi approves of us," he whispered to Darcy as Taylor walked ahead of them toward the exit.

"I'm sure the rules are in place to protect people," Darcy said.

Mike stopped and faced her. "You're really okay with this?" he asked.

"I am. A little shaken, I guess. But only because this has brought back so many memories of that day…." She let the words trail away, determined not to dwell on the sadness. "Seeing Taylor so happy and healthy, and knowing I had a part in that helps more than I would have thought."

"Thank you," Mike said. "The words aren't enough, and they can't possibly convey the depth of my gratitude, but they're all I know to say."

"You're welcome. I kept the letter you wrote to me. Not Taylor's—the one the Donor Alliance forwarded to me right after the transplant." The letter had been short and to the point.

"I don't even remember what I wrote. I was still in such a fog after everything that had happened. And Taylor was still a very sick little girl then."

Darcy wondered at the miracle of all of this—not just the miracle of Riley's heart beating in this girl's chest, but the miracle of their learning the truth. Had there been a divine hand at work in bringing them together? She'd started the dance class as a way to bring children into her life, but never dreamed she'd bring in this particular child. That was another kind of miracle, that Darcy would have a chance to be a part of Taylor's life, even if it was only for a couple of hours one afternoon a week.

And then there was Taylor's father—a handsome, overprotective, enigmatic and intriguing man. He would of necessity be part of Darcy's life now, too. The thought was a warm ember in a heart that had been cold too long. Looking at him now, seeing his genuine concern, she felt a little less lonely than she had before.

WHEN TAYLOR HUGGED her in greeting the next Wednesday afternoon, Darcy felt a special warmth in the embrace. She fought the urge to cling to the girl too long, to listen to the steady beat of the little heart and remember her son.

"I told my mom all about you," Taylor said. "She wants to meet you."

"I'd be happy to meet her." She was curious about the woman who had divorced a man like Mike. The more she saw of the handsome pediatrician, the better her picture of a devoted father. Had he been a less devoted husband? Or was some other fatal flaw lurking beneath the handsome, caring facade?

"Can you come to dinner at my house this weekend?" Taylor asked.

"Your house?"

"Yeah. She said that would be easier. Her apartment's really small and besides, she doesn't cook."

Wasn't that what restaurants were for? "And

your dad is okay with us meeting at your house?" she asked.

"Dad doesn't mind. Mom eats with us all the time."

"All right," Darcy said. What business was it of hers if Mike dined regularly with his ex. After all, the woman was the mother of his child. It was probably great for Taylor that her parents got along so well. "I'm working Friday evening, but I can come Saturday."

"Great." Taylor's eyes shone. "I can't wait."

Darcy was nervous at the thought of sitting down face-to-face with Mike and his ex. They'd want to talk about the transplant, of course, and about Riley and the circumstances of his death. She'd have to work hard to keep it together. But maybe talking with two sympathetic adults would help her. They, of all people, would come closest to understanding her pain. And she'd have Taylor there to remind her that some good had come of her sacrifice.

For the next forty-five minutes, the girls tried out their moves and learned new ones. The studio echoed with their laughter and shouts as they turned and swayed, dipped and shook. They sang along with the songs they knew and made up words to new ones. Taylor turned out to have a wicked sense of humor, and a knack for outrageous rhymes. "The boys all think I'm such a cutie, when they see me shake my booty," she rapped, shaking her hips for emphasis.

She quickly looked at Darcy. "Don't tell my dad I said that," she said. "He'd be horrified."

No doubt. "My lips are sealed," Darcy promised.

Toward the end of class, the talk turned once more to costumes. "My mom found this pink fabric with glitter all over it," Hannah said.

"I want a red costume," Debby said. "With lots of fringe."

"I'm trying to talk my mom into buying me silver pants," Zoe said.

Only Taylor failed to chime in. She'd fallen silent, her expression glum.

Since Mike appeared to be late today, Darcy waited until the other girls had departed with their mothers before she asked Taylor if she felt all right. "You got so quiet suddenly," she said. "What's wrong?"

Taylor lifted one shoulder in half a shrug.

"You were fine when you got here," Darcy persisted. "Did one of your meds make you not feel well?"

"I'm worried about my costume," Taylor admitted.

"Your costume? Honey, you've got six weeks. I'm sure you can come up with a very nice one by then. I'll help you."

Taylor shook her head. "I'm not worried about *finding* one, I'm worried about *wearing* one."

Darcy knelt so that she was eye level with the girl. "I don't understand."

Taylor pulled at the blue turtleneck sweater she wore. "I have a scar from my surgery," she said. "A big one."

Darcy swallowed hard. "Can I see?"

Taylor nodded and pulled up the hem of her sweater. Darcy struggled not to reveal the shock she felt at seeing the pink, puckered scar that bisected the child's torso from neck to navel. She stared at the spot near the center of Taylor's chest. Riley's heart was in there. *Taylor's heart*, she corrected herself.

"That is a big scar," she said, tugging the sweater back into place. "But as you get older, it will fade—and you'll get bigger, so it will seem smaller. In the meantime, I'll help you come up with something to wear that will hide that scar."

"But belly dancers have to show their bellies."

"Says who?" Darcy stood. "Did you know that in Egypt—where belly dancing started—it's actually *illegal* for dancers to show their stomachs?"

"It is? That's silly."

"Sometimes rules are silly, but it also shows that you can dance real belly dance and not show much of your body at all."

"I just don't want to look different," she said.

"You'll be beautiful, I promise." Darcy was determined that Taylor would leave here today feeling better about her body and about dancing. After all, that was one of her aims in teaching this girls' class. "The important thing to remember when dancing is to not think about the people watching you or what they think or feel," she said. "It's all about how dancing makes *you* feel."

"How do you feel when you dance?" Taylor asked.

"I feel I have a healthy body and can move and am alive. I listen to the music and try to forget about everything else except losing myself in the beauty of this one moment." It was dance's power to help her forget that had saved her in the agonizing days and months after Riley's and Pete's deaths.

"How can I forget other people if I'm performing for them?" Taylor asked.

"They only think you're performing for them," Darcy said. "The secret is, you're really dancing for yourself. You're doing this for you."

"That's what I wanted to tell my dad when he was worried about me coming here," Taylor said. "But I don't think he'd understand."

"Dads don't always understand. But that's okay. He let you come to class after all," she said. "So he must be getting better about not being so overprotective."

"Maybe." She sighed. "It would be easier if he had a girlfriend or something. You know, if he had someone else to worry about besides me."

So Mike didn't have a girlfriend? A single, good-looking doctor? Darcy ignored the flutter in her chest at the thought. What was so unusual about that, anyway? She didn't have a man in her life. She didn't want one. She liked making her own decisions and not having to rely on or be responsible for anyone else. "I don't think a girlfriend would keep your father from being concerned about you," she said. "And tell the truth—you'd miss it if he didn't fuss over you some."

"Some. I just wish...I wish sometimes he didn't fuss so much."

The door opened and there was the man himself, looking harried. "Sorry I'm late," he said. "I got behind at the office."

"That's all right." Darcy rested her hand on Taylor's shoulder. "It gave Taylor and me more time to talk. She's concerned about what costume she'll wear in our show. I promised to help her put something together. If that's all right." She didn't want Mike to think she was overstepping her role. "Or maybe her mother would like to make something..."

He shook his head. "Melissa isn't the domestic type. And her schedule is so hectic she might not have time to shop before the show."

"Darcy can come to dinner Saturday," Taylor said.

"I hope it wasn't too short notice," Mike said. "Melissa just let me know she's going to be in town."

"No, that's fine." She'd never known a woman who had willingly given up custody of her child. If she and Pete had divorced, she would never have surrendered custody of Riley to him.

But theirs had been a different situation. Pete wasn't responsible like Mike. He couldn't be trusted to put his son's welfare ahead of every other consideration.

He'd proved that when he'd taken the boy out on the night of their deaths. When Darcy had left them that evening, Pete had intended to stay home. He'd been drinking, as he did every evening he didn't work, but he hadn't been drunk. Darcy had trusted him to look after their son.

After Darcy had left, a friend had called and invited Pete out. Pete, always ready for a party, had set out in a snowstorm, Riley in the backseat of the car. He'd lost control on the icy road, plunging them over a cliff to their deaths.

If only Darcy had stayed home that evening. If only she'd insisted Pete stay home. If only she'd been harder on him about his drinking… She closed her eyes against the familiar guilty litany. Pete's drinking and driving had killed their son, but Darcy's irresponsibility in leaving her son in the care of a man she knew was an alcoholic made her just as responsible. She'd been given the greatest gift a person could have, the gift of a child, and she'd screwed up. She could never forget, and she could never atone for that mistake.

The prospect of dinner with Taylor and her parents was both a welcome change and a concern. Darcy looked forward to good conversation and a meal that wasn't microwaved, but she hoped she could get through the evening without too many sad memories intruding. She was curious to observe the relationship between Mike and his ex. Was the handsome doctor still single because he was carrying a torch for his ex, or had marriage to her turned him off the idea altogether?

Saturday afternoon, she took her time getting ready for the outing, and was putting the finishing touches on her makeup when someone pounded on her door, startling her.

"Hey, sis." Dave greeted her with a bear hug when she opened the door. "Don't you look nice." He sniffed. "You smell nice, too. You dancing somewhere tonight?"

"That's not a dancing outfit." A woman with shoulder-length auburn hair peered around Dave's broad back.

"Carrie!" Darcy hugged the woman. "It's good to see you."

"It's good to see you, too. And Dave's right, you look fantastic." Carrie stepped back, surveying Darcy's jeans and sweater combo. The sweater was a bright ruby-red scoop neck with three-quarter sleeves. She wore simple hoop earrings and a ruby heart pendant on a gold chain. "Do you have a date?" Carrie asked.

"A date? No!" Darcy felt her face heat. "One of my dance students invited me to dinner."

"Since when does a dance student make you blush like that?" Dave asked.

"Maybe this student has a handsome single brother," Carrie said.

"The student is ten years old," Darcy explained. "She's in a new class I'm teaching for girls."

"How sweet," Carrie said. "I bet they're just adorable. Will they dance at your student recital in the spring?"

"Absolutely," Darcy said, relieved the subject had turned away from her plans for the evening. "They really are a great group of girls."

"We won't keep you," Dave said. "I just stopped by to return your snowblower."

"It's fixed?" Darcy asked.

"No, I'm returning it broken." He punched her arm, though not too hard. "Of course it's fixed. You want me to leave it in front of the garage?"

"That'll be fine. Just make sure there's room for my students to get around it."

Carrie and Darcy moved into the living room after Dave went back outside. "A kids' class is such a good idea," Carrie said. "If you ever need any help with it, let me know."

"I might take you up on that offer," Darcy said. "You could help with costumes, maybe."

Carrie glanced out the window, toward where Dave was unloading the snowblower from his truck.

"I really love children, but I'm not sure how Dave feels about them. What do you think?"

Darcy's stomach tightened at the not-so-casual question. She loved Carrie, and her brother's refusal to commit to her after five years was frustrating, but her loyalty was to Dave. "I don't know, Carrie," she said. "I'm not the one you should be asking. Talk to him."

Carrie turned from the window. "But it's a touchy subject. If I bring up children, he'll think I'm pressuring him to get married. That's why we split up the last time."

"I didn't know that." She tried hard not to pry, and Dave had kept silent, either to avoid burdening her further in her grief or to protect himself.

"He says the men and women in your family aren't cut out for marriage," Carrie said. "He can list every divorce or failed relationship for every one of his relatives going back three generations. I can see how those kind of statistics could make a person wary, but it didn't stop you."

"No, it didn't," Darcy agreed. She'd been determined to break their family curse, but she hadn't succeeded.

"I sometimes wonder if it isn't really marriage," Carrie said. "If it's just me. Maybe I'm not the person he wants to spend the rest of his life with."

"Dave loves you," Darcy said. "He was miserable while you were apart."

"I was miserable, too. But I want children. And I'm not getting any younger. I don't know what to do."

Darcy squeezed Carrie's arm in a gesture of comfort. "Talk to him. Tell him how you feel."

"You're right. I just have to find the right time."

The door opened and the sound of Dave stamping snow from his feet echoed through the house. Such a masculine sound, Darcy thought. She had a flashback to a snowy afternoon a few years before, Pete coming in from work, knocking the snow off his boots, enveloping her in a hug, his cheek cold against hers, his arms squeezing her so tight…

She shook away the memory, the vividness of it making her chest hurt. How long before emotions would stop ambushing her this way?

"You're all set," Dave said when the women returned to the kitchen. "Call me if it gives you any more trouble."

"Thanks for fixing the snowblower," she said.

"No problem." He took Carrie's coat from the peg by the door and offered it to her. "We won't keep you. Have a good time on your date."

"It's not a date," she protested.

He laughed. "Whatever you say." He leaned over and kissed her cheek.

"You know I will." She wouldn't have gotten through the past two years without Dave's help. His physical help with things like the snowblower and moving heavy furniture, and his calm, steadying presence in her life, reassuring her that she could go on.

But there were some things a brother couldn't do.

He couldn't teach her how to create a new life that looked so different from the one she'd lost.

CHAPTER FOUR

WHILE MIKE MARINATED STEAKS, Taylor set the table for four. All day she'd bounced like a pinball from one activity to another, excited over the prospect of Darcy coming for dinner. Her mood was contagious, and Mike found himself glancing at the clock every three minutes, listening for a knock on the door. Darcy would arrive first. Melissa was only ever on time for work. When they'd been married, it used to drive him nuts that she never missed a flight when she was almost always late for everything else *but* work.

"Dad, we should have bought flowers for the table." Taylor rushed from the dining room to the kitchen.

"I didn't think of it, sweetheart, but it will be all right."

"Flowers would make the table look more special," she said.

Did she want things special for Darcy, or for her mother? Or special because her parents were dining together, something they didn't ordinarily do? Mike had heard of children who clung to the belief their divorced parents would reunite, though Taylor had never expressed any such desire. Still, it would be natural for her to want that, wouldn't it?

If Mike had had his wish, he and Melissa would never have divorced. Not because he still believed she was the love of his life—that belief had died in the bitter fights near the end. But he came from a family where marriage was for life. Even imperfect partners stayed together, because they'd promised to do so. Part of being an adult was accepting that life wasn't all hearts and roses.

But Melissa had felt differently. Maybe she thought she could find the romance she was missing with someone else. Mike certainly hadn't made her happy, and she'd half convinced him he didn't have what it took to be a good partner to any woman. "Darcy and your mother are both coming to see you," he said. "I'm sure they won't even notice if there aren't any flowers."

"Do you think I look okay?" Taylor asked.

Mike set down the fork he'd been using to turn the steaks. He didn't know whether it was her age or a consequence of her surgery, but lately Taylor had been more concerned with her appearance, a trend that troubled him. "You're beautiful," he said. "And that purple sweater looks great on you." The cowl neck framed her face and effectively covered her scar. She wore it over dark jeans and purple suede booties her mother had given her for Christmas.

His praise eased the frown lines on the girl's

forehead, but they soon returned as she studied him. "You're not very dressed up," she said.

He supposed this was the ten-year-old version of the adult female's *You're not going to wear that, are you?* He glanced down at his khaki trousers and pale blue button-down shirt. "What's wrong with this outfit?"

"You look like you're going to the office. You should wear your new shirt."

The new shirt was another attempt by Taylor to update his wardrobe. It featured maroon, blue and gold stripes with thin metallic threads woven through. "Nick Jonas has one almost just like it," Taylor had solemnly informed him when he'd unwrapped it. He'd worn it one night, at home, to placate her, and then had hidden it at the back of his closet. "Honey, don't you think that shirt's a bit too…flashy for a simple dinner at home?"

Her expression clearly conveyed that Dad was clueless. "Darcy likes flashy," she said. "Her dance costumes are colorful and glittery. Wear the shirt. Please!"

Mike decided that giving in to Taylor was easier than trying to convince her otherwise. And if she could focus on his appearance maybe she wouldn't worry so much about her own looks.

Changing shirts also meant changing pants. He decided on dark blue jeans, since all his dress pants looked ridiculous with the stripes. He was buttoning the sleeves and frowning at his reflection in the bathroom mirror when the doorbell rang. "She's here!" Taylor shouted, and thundered across the room.

Mike arrived at the front door in time to help Darcy out of her coat. "I hope you didn't have any trouble finding the place," he said.

"Not at all."

"You look great," Taylor said of Darcy's jeans and red sweater.

"So do you," she said. "I love that turtleneck, and those boots are to die for."

Taylor grinned and tugged up the legs of her jeans to show them off. "Thanks. My mom gave them to me for Christmas."

"She obviously has good taste." Darcy turned to Mike. "Nice shirt," she said. He was alert for any hint of mockery in her voice, or some sign of sarcasm in her eyes but found none. Did that mean she really liked the shirt—on him?

"I brought wine," she said, and offered a wrapped bottle, which turned out to contain a very nice merlot. "The clerk at the liquor store recommended it."

"It'll go great with the steaks," he said. "Thank you."

She looked around expectantly. "Melissa isn't here yet," Mike said.

"Mom's always late," Taylor added.

Mike hung Darcy's coat in the closet and trailed

her and Taylor into the living room. "Let me show you the house," Taylor said. "My room is down here."

As they proceeded down the hallway, Mike detoured to the kitchen to start the stove-top grill for the steaks. He opened the wine and poured two glasses and waited.

And waited. The house wasn't that large—where could Taylor have taken Darcy? Was she stuck in Taylor's room, playing Barbies and too polite to extricate herself?

He started down the hallway and soon heard voices. They weren't coming from Taylor's room, but from his.

"This is my dad's bathroom," Taylor was saying. "It's usually really messy in here. This is the cologne I gave him for his birthday…"

Darcy turned from the doorway of the bathroom when he entered the bedroom. "Taylor wanted to show me everything," she said. "I told her we shouldn't invade your privacy, but she insisted."

Her smile added to his embarrassment. He picked up the clothes he'd discarded earlier and tossed them on the bed, which at least he'd taken the trouble to make up that morning. "I guess it's not like you haven't seen a man's bedroom before." He wanted to take the words back as soon as he'd said them. Did she think he was implying something risqué—that she'd seen a lot of men's bedrooms?

Had she?

"Hmm." She looked around the room, at the cherry bed and dresser Melissa had picked out, and the bookcase full of paperback thrillers and suspense novels that served as a nightstand. "It's been a while."

It had been a while since a woman who wasn't his housekeeper had been in this room, too. He felt the same way he had when he'd watched Darcy dance, that awareness of himself as a man without a woman in his life, and of her as a desirable, sexy woman. "Come on, Taylor, let's go back into the living room," he said. "Supper's almost ready."

"I have one more thing to show Darcy," Taylor said. "I almost forgot." She ran to the dresser and picked up a framed photograph. "This is me, right after I got my new heart."

The picture had been taken only a few hours posttransplant. The girl in the hospital bed was dwarfed by the machines around her, tubes and wires trailing out of her. Despite all this, the image was precious to Mike because Taylor was pink cheeked and smiling, a marked contrast to the sad, blue-tinged girl she'd been only hours before.

Darcy stared at the picture and all color left her face. She opened her mouth as if to speak, but no words came out. Alarmed, Mike took the picture from her. She swayed, and he put his arm around her to steady her. "Are you okay?" he asked.

"Yes, I..." She tried to smile, but the expression

was more of a grimace. "I didn't recognize you, Taylor," she said. "You look so...so healthy now."

"Taylor, put the picture back on the dresser." Mike handed it to his daughter and steered Darcy toward the door, still supporting her with his arm. "Let's go into the living room and sit down. There are a couple of glasses of wine on the counter in the kitchen. Taylor, why don't you get those for us."

Taylor raced ahead while her father and Darcy made their way slowly down the hall. "I'm sorry," Mike said. "I didn't think about how much of a shock that picture can be. As a doctor I forget."

"No, it's okay." She was still very pale, but her voice was stronger. "I just…" She shook her head.

They sat and Taylor brought the wine. After a few sips, Darcy's color returned. "Thanks," she said.

"Are you okay?" Taylor asked, eyes wide, lower lip trembling.

Darcy squeezed her hand. "Come sit here with me and tell me what you did today."

While the two talked, Mike returned to the kitchen to finish preparing dinner. It didn't take much imagination to realize the kinds of memories that picture must have conjured—memories of her son in a similar hospital bed, hooked to similar machinery, before he died.

It was also easy for him to imagine how the revelation of Taylor's identity as the donation recipient had hurt her, as she'd been forced to relive the circumstances that had led to the donation.

"Is everything okay?" he called. Maybe he should go back into the living room….

"I'm fine," Darcy answered. She sounded stronger. "What are you making?"

"Steaks. How do you like yours cooked?"

"Well-done."

"That's the only way Daddy will let me eat mine," Taylor said. "He says there could be germs or something in undercooked meat, but then he eats his steak all pink in the middle. Yuck."

Mike shook his head. He and Taylor were going to have to have a talk about boundaries and what constituted proper conversation with strangers.

The doorbell rang again. Mike let Taylor answer it, and heard Melissa greeting her daughter. He wiped his hands on a napkin and went to begin what he hoped wouldn't be another awkward evening balanced between the adoration of his daughter and the judgment of his ex-wife.

THE FORMER MRS. MIKE CARTER was tall and beautiful, with stylishly cut dark brown hair, and expensive boots and coat. "I can't believe you're wearing that shirt," she said to Mike as he stepped into the living room. She laughed, the sound loud in the sudden stillness.

"It's a beautiful shirt," protested Taylor, who stood between her parents in the entryway.

"Yes, it is, dear, but it's *so* not your father." Melissa turned and noticed Darcy, who was still seated on the sofa.

Darcy set aside her wineglass and stood. "I'm Darcy O'Connor," she said, moving forward, hand outstretched. "It's so nice to meet you."

"I can't tell you how much I've looked forward to meeting you," Melissa said, gripping Darcy's hand firmly. "All I've heard since Taylor started classes was Darcy this and Darcy that. And then to find out you're the mother of that dear boy who gave her his heart—it's just too amazing."

Darcy tried not to wince. It wasn't as if Riley had voluntarily handed over his heart to Taylor.

"Can I get you some wine?" Mike asked Melissa.

"Yes, please." She settled on the sofa next to Darcy, Taylor on her other side. "So you're a belly dancer," she said. "Such an unusual occupation. And you really make a living dancing?"

"Dancing and teaching. And I sometimes do temp work to bring in extra money." Darcy could tell by the way Melissa's nose wrinkled that she didn't think much of Darcy's financially precarious lifestyle, and her next words confirmed it.

"I suppose you artists don't really care that much

about money," she said. "I could never live that way. I've grown too used to my luxuries, I suppose."

By the time Mike called them to the table, Melissa had revealed her current relationship with a senior pilot and described her latest shopping trip in Paris.

"That sounds wonderful," Darcy said, continuing the conversation as they took their seats, she to Mike's left, with Taylor on his other side and Melissa at the opposite end of the table.

"Even though I wear a uniform to work, I like to look my best in my off hours," Melissa said.

Darcy purchased most of her clothes from thrift stores and the sale racks at discount merchants. "I'll admit, I don't worry much about clothes," she said. "Except for my costumes."

"Darcy has some lovely costumes," Taylor said. "All silky and shimmery with all kinds of jewels and sequins."

"Not much call for that sort of thing in my line of work," Melissa said with a chuckle.

"Darcy dances at a restaurant sometimes," Taylor said. "What was the name of it again? I want to come see you there."

"Arabica. They serve Middle Eastern food. It's very good."

Taylor looked skeptical. "I've never had Middle Eastern food before."

"It's different, but good," Darcy said. "Though not as good as this steak, I'm sure."

"Mike always was a good cook," Melissa said. "I never wanted to waste the little spare time I had in the kitchen. With my travel schedule I have to eat out too much. But the other night I had dinner in the most fabulous restaurant in Naples…."

Darcy was able to enjoy her steak in relative silence, as Melissa took over the lion's share of the conversation, segueing from a description of the menu at the Naples restaurant to a long story about her latest trip to Antwerp. Taylor watched her mother with adoring eyes. Why didn't Melissa pay more attention to the girl? Why didn't she ask her daughter about school or dancing, to include her in the conversation? The one time Taylor tried to share something that had happened in class, Melissa turned the conversation back to herself.

As for Mike, he focused on his plate. What had this quiet, solemn man ever seen in this outgoing, self-centered woman?

At that moment, Mike looked up and met Darcy's gaze. A spark of unmistakable warmth lit his eyes. "Let me get you some more wine," he said, leaning forward to refill her glass. She waved him away.

"I should have warned you, I'm a real lightweight when it comes to alcohol. I can only have one glass if I'm going to drive home later."

"You could just spend the night here," Taylor said. "In my room."

Melissa's laughter was too loud, and Darcy felt

her face heat. "That would be fun, but I need to get home."

The awkward silence stretched only a few moments before Taylor came to their rescue. "Next Saturday my mom is taking me to Disney On Ice."

"Is that the one with all the Disney princesses?" Darcy asked. "And the Olympic champions?"

"Yes. I can't wait. I always watch all the ice-skating at the Olympics. It's so beautiful."

"I'm able to get tickets through the airline," Melissa said. "It's one of the perks of my job."

"I wanted to go last year, but Mom wasn't in town," Taylor said. "And Dad didn't want to take me in such a big crowd—that germ thing." She made a face. "He still doesn't really want me to go, but now that they're not married anymore, he can't tell Mom what to do."

"I never told your mother what to do before," Mike said.

"Your father is not that dumb," Melissa said. The words were complimentary, but her tone imbued them with a sting. Darcy cringed.

"What will you wear to the show?" Darcy quickly asked Taylor.

The rest of the meal was filled with talk of clothes, from the story of how Mike had come to own a Jonas Brothers–style shirt to Darcy's various dance costumes.

By the time Mike announced dessert, Darcy was

feeling more relaxed. Melissa wasn't the type of woman she'd normally have befriended—she was too brittle and self-centered—but she clearly loved her daughter and had the facile charm of someone used to navigating a variety of social situations.

"What are we having for dessert?" Melissa asked as Mike cleared the table.

"Strawberry tart."

"From Michelson's? That was always my favorite."

"Taylor's, too," he said drily. He caught Darcy's eye and she had to bite the inside of her cheek to keep from laughing.

With dessert, Melissa had more wine—too much wine, Darcy thought. Her teasing tone with Mike took on a harder edge. "He's a better cook than I was and he certainly makes more money," she said at one point. "Taylor and I will have to put our heads together and see if we can't find him some equally studious teacher or librarian, someone who will appreciate his good qualities."

"I'm sure plenty of women appreciate Mike," Darcy murmured.

"You, for instance?" Melissa laughed before Darcy could answer, as if the idea was ridiculous.

Across the table, Mike looked ready to spit nails. Darcy rose. "Thank you for the lovely dinner," she said. "I really should be going now." She nodded to Melissa. "It was nice to meet you."

Mike made no protest. "Thank you for coming," he said as he walked her to the door.

"I had a nice time," she said. "And it was nice to meet Taylor's mother."

"I'll make sure she takes a cab home," he said. "She doesn't always behave like this."

"It's fine. You don't have to apologize."

She hurried to her car, wanting nothing more than to be home in her pajamas, her hand wrapped around a mug of tea. She'd need more than flannel pj's and tea to soothe her, though. The evening had shaken her—starting with Taylor dragging her into Mike's bedroom. Yes, it was just a room, but seeing his books on the nightstand, his clothes on the floor and his razor on the edge of the sink had felt so intimate. It made him less intimidating, more accessible.

When he'd joined them in the bedroom, she'd felt the attraction between them heating up.

But that picture of Taylor in the hospital had been like a whole refrigerator truck of ice dumped on her. Seeing the child connected to all those machines—the way Riley had looked the last time she'd seen him—had jerked her back to that moment of horror.

And now she'd run away from him and from his happy family. No, he and Melissa were no longer married, but they had a child they both clearly loved. A happy, but fragile child who took handfuls of pills multiple times a day and who was one bad cold away from ending up back in the hospital, hooked up to those awful machines. Darcy shuddered at the thought. She wasn't ready for that. No matter how much she was attracted to a man, she would never be ready for that again.

CHAPTER FIVE

Mike hated the weekends Taylor spent with her mother. He tried to fill the hours with work, but more often than not dealing with other sick children only heightened his worry over Taylor. Not that he didn't trust Melissa to look after their daughter, but she wasn't a medical professional. She might not realize something was wrong until it was too late.

This was the weekend of the long-awaited Disney On Ice spectacular. "I'm really too old for this," Taylor had confided to Mike as she'd packed for the weekend away. "I mean, I'd rather go to a concert or something. Hannah Montana's coming to town."

"Is that a hint?" he asked.

She grinned. "Maybe. Anyway, Mom wants to go to this, so I guess it will be all right."

Mike knew she was secretly excited about the show, with all its glitter and glamour and exaltation of everything princess. She wore her purple boots and, at the last minute, had added a sparkling tiara someone had given her in the hospital.

The hospital made him think of Brent. The boy had been back in the office this afternoon. Mike had changed his medication and ordered a blood workup, but he was worried. Every sick child was a potential Taylor. Mike didn't want to make the same mistake with others he'd made with her. Was he missing something that might turn out worse because of his oversight? Should he send the boy to a specialist, and if so, which one?

He continued to ponder this as he made his rounds at the hospital Friday evening. He only had two patients to see: a girl recovering from pneumonia and a boy who'd crashed his dirt bike at a racetrack. Both were doing well and Mike left the hospital in a good mood.

Usually on nights when Mike had the house to himself, he indulged in takeout and beer while watching a ball game or a movie on TV. But there was no game on tonight, and no movie he wanted to see.

Maybe he'd go out to eat. Someplace nice. The kind of place he'd take a date, if he dated.

As he drove away from the hospital, he kept an eye out for a likely looking restaurant. He'd order a good steak, and one glass of red wine. Then a red neon sign caught his eye and he tapped the brake. *Arabica*. The restaurant where Darcy danced. Not giving himself time to change his mind, he put on his blinker and turned into the parking lot.

He asked for a table near the small space at the front of the room that served as a stage. He ordered lamb kebabs and a Scotch and water and waited until the lights dimmed. The sounds of flutes and drums and a woman singing in Arabic filled the room.

Darcy arrived in a swirl of purple and gold, sparkling with sequins and jewels. A many-paneled skirt hung low on her hips, framed by a jeweled, fringed girdle. A jewel glinted at her navel and more fringe trimmed the bra from which the tops of her breasts spilled. Mike had a flash of memory of the first time he'd seen her dance, that day in her studio, when the air around him had seemed charged and he'd realized how empty his life was of all things sexual.

As the music rose now she began to shimmy, the fringe and sequins shuddering, her flesh quivering, mesmerizing him. She moved in time with the music, first fast, then slow, tracing arcs and circles in the air with her hips, then her breasts, making the fringe jump and dance along with her. She undulated with snakelike grace, then pranced across the stage, hips bouncing provocatively. All the while she seduced the audience with her smile and teased them with her eyes. They cheered and whistled and applauded. One man's voice rose over the others. "Baby, you are gorgeous!"

Mike craned his head, trying to find the guy in the crowd.

The music switched to a more modern rock number and she vamped, acting out the words of the song, in which the singer chided her man for not treating her right. She promised to make him pay for his mistakes and find a man who would treat her like a queen. Mike had no doubt she'd have plenty of willing candidates in this room if she issued an invitation.

The music changed again and she ventured into the audience, moving among the tables, stopping to dance for appreciative diners. At one table she invited a young girl to join her, applauding as the girl twisted and shimmied. Mike thought of Taylor, and how quickly she and Darcy had hit it off. Darcy had an easy way with children, and Taylor, who so often missed her mother, basked in attention from an adult female who was equal parts fantasy princess and mentor.

She moved on, twirling and gliding, and stopped directly in front of Mike. As her eyes met his, he felt certain she'd been aware of his presence for some time, and had deliberately sought him out.

The music slowed and she slowed with it, her moves becoming more controlled. More sensual. The two of them might have been alone in the room, for all Mike noticed the people around them. The exotic music and the seductive sight and scent of her filled his senses. He was no longer a single dad and doctor....

Then the spell was broken by a man who inserted himself between them. "Come dance with me, honey," the man said. He wiggled his hips and laughed.

Darcy tried to move away from him, but he grasped her arm. "Wait. I've got something for you."

He reached into his pocket and pulled out a crumpled bill and tried to stuff it into her top.

Mike was out of his chair and had a hold of the man before he realized what he was doing. The guy released Darcy and turned toward Mike. Mike landed a blow on the jaw, then watched as the man sank to his knees and toppled over with a groan.

The next thing he knew, Darcy was dragging him out of the dining room and down a dimly lit corridor. "What are you doing?" he protested. "I haven't paid for my dinner. What about the rest of your show?"

"The show's over. And don't worry about your dinner. I'll talk to Dileep." She opened the door to a storage room that apparently doubled as her dressing room, dragged him inside and shut it firmly behind them.

He stood with his back against the door, breathing hard, his hand throbbing. She stood a scant foot away, arms folded under her breasts, her accentuated cleavage and bright costume in sharp contrast to her disapproving schoolmarm expression. "Well?" she said.

"Well what?" He rubbed his throbbing hand.

"Why did you hit him?"

"I'd think that would be obvious."

"I would have handled him. Dileep was already on his way to help."

"Who is Dileep?"

"The owner. He doesn't like this kind of disruption."

Such a polite word for a brawl, or what would have been a brawl if the other guy hadn't toppled like a tree. "Does this sort of thing happen often?" Mike asked.

"Occasionally. Usually the guy's had too much to drink. I put him off and Dileep escorts him away and suggests he leave and not worry about paying for his dinner. Most of the other diners never notice anything's wrong."

Mike was pretty sure at least half the room had seen him deck the guy. "I'm sorry," he said. "I wasn't thinking. I just saw his hands on you and..." He shook his head.

She uncrossed her arms. "You surprised me. I didn't think you were the type to do something like that."

"I'm not. At least, not usually." He grimaced.

"Is your hand all right?"

"It's not broken, but it smarts. Serves me right for pulling such a stunt."

"Let me see."

"No, it's fine. Really." But she took his hand, cradling it in hers. Her nails were painted a bright pink, her fingers long and slender. She held him gently, her skin soft and warm as only a woman's could be. He was a man alone with a beautiful woman he suddenly wanted very much.

The strength of his desire surprised him as much as the punch had. Tonight was obviously an evening for every long-suppressed emotion to rise to the surface, so he didn't fight the feeling, merely brought his free hand to rest against the exquisite tenderness of the hollow of her throat.

When her eyes met his, questioning, he brought his lips to hers. Answering the question.

Her lips were as soft as he'd imagined, and as warm and welcoming as he'd hoped. She arched into him, and he put his hand at the curve of her waist to steady her, his palm resting against her bare skin.

There was no hesitation or awkwardness in this kiss, no fumbling of strangers. Her lips parted in invitation and he accepted. She tasted sweet and earthy, like everything sex should be.

He kissed until he was breathless, reluctant to break the spell of the moment. Then he realized she was trembling, and he was trembling too. He raised his head but kept his hand at her waist. "If you want me to apologize for that, I won't."

"No. No, I don't want you to apologize." She rested her palm against his chest, her cheeks flushed, her breasts rising and falling with each breath. They stared at each other, the amazement he felt reflected in her eyes.

Finally, she took a step back. "Let me change clothes and we'll go somewhere and talk."

He waited for her in the hall. While he was

standing there a burly man in a dark suit approached. "Is Darcy in there?" he asked.

"Are you Dileep?"

"Dileep Aswan."

"Darcy's changing. I'm sorry about tonight. I'll pay for my meal, and for that man's, too. And any other damages." He reached for his wallet.

"No, no." Dileep waved him away. "I have a wife and three daughters. I understand how it is." His expression grew more stern. "But don't come to watch her dance anymore. Some men can sit back and watch others admire their woman, but you cannot. I cannot. We're too hot-blooded, so we must stay away."

Mike had never in his life thought of himself as hot-blooded, but he nodded. "Yes. I'll stay away. I promise."

When Darcy emerged a few moments later, dressed in jeans and a red parka, Mike told her he'd spoken to Dileep.

"I heard," she said.

"He seemed more amused than anything, as if I'd done what any man would."

"You didn't tell him I wasn't your woman."

"Explaining seemed too complicated." After the kiss they'd just shared, he wasn't sure how he'd characterize their relationship. He'd punched a man because of Darcy, then kissed her passionately—it seemed clear they'd moved beyond casual friendship, though he could think of half a dozen reasons why this was a bad idea. "Where do you want to go now?" he asked.

"There's a coffee shop two doors down. Let's go there."

She left her costume in her car and they walked down to the coffee shop. At this time of night it was quiet. She ordered a chai latte and Mike asked for black coffee. Now that the adrenaline had faded he was starting to drag.

They sat at a table near the front windows. In the harsh fluorescent lighting the stage makeup she'd worn to dance looked overdone, like a girl playing dress-up. "I usually go straight home after I dance," she said, as if reading his thoughts.

"I usually fall asleep on the sofa in front of the television on the nights Taylor's away."

"Tonight was certainly more exciting than that."

"I'm sorry I overreacted with that guy. I didn't mean to embarrass you or get you in trouble with the owner."

"It's okay. By next Friday it'll be forgotten."

"I think Dileep may have the wrong impression now about our relationship. I hope that's not going to be a problem. I mean, if you have a boyfriend…" He had a sudden image of some big bruiser looking him up and warning him away.

"I don't have a boyfriend," she said. "Don't worry."

"I'm not really at a place in my life where I want

to date anyone, either," he said. Better to be honest with her, in case she expected that kiss to lead to something more. As much as the physical pleasure of kissing her might lead him to wish they could take things further, he wasn't one for casual affairs, and his failed marriage proved he wasn't good at emotional entanglements. "It's only in the past few months I've felt comfortable letting Taylor out of my sight for more than a few hours."

"Is her health really that fragile?"

"So far she's progressing remarkably well. But the best way to deal with setbacks is to anticipate them." If he'd anticipated problems earlier on he might have been able to spare Taylor so much of the suffering she'd gone through.

"I guess I'd be overprotective in your situation, too."

"Melissa says I go too far. She was always able to detach better than I was." He took a long drink of coffee. When he'd met Melissa, he'd been drawn to her energy and drive. Her confidence had been contagious. Later, after Taylor became ill, he saw her darker side. "As you might have noticed, she can be a bit self-centered. I suppose I let her get away with too much. I hate to fight in front of Taylor."

"She wasn't the only reason I left last night," Darcy said.

He'd wondered…. "That picture upset you. The one of Taylor in the hospital."

She nodded. "It looked so much like Riley the last time I saw him. Except he was already dead. Brain-dead, anyway. The machines were just keeping his organs healthy until they could be donated."

"Losing your husband at the same time must have made everything ten times worse."

"Yes." She gripped her cup with both hands and sipped her tea.

"Are you able to talk about this?" he asked. "We can change the subject."

"No, I'm okay. It's good, really, to talk to someone."

"Tell me about your husband, then. What was he like?"

"Pete was…he was charismatic. The kind of guy who made friends easily. We met while I was at the University of Colorado." She smiled. "He gave me a traffic ticket, then called the next day and asked me out."

"He was a cop?"

"Yes. And I was a very serious postgraduate student, working on my master's degree in community relations."

His surprise must have shown on his face. She laughed again. "I know. What happened to that woman? A friend talked me into taking a belly dance class and I was hooked. By that time, Pete and I were pretty serious. I told him I wanted to quit school and become a dancer and he urged me to go for it. That's when I knew he was a keeper. We got married a few months later."

Mike was sure he would have told her she was crazy to abandon her education.

"You know what they say about too good to be true," she said. "That was Pete. I didn't realize until after we'd married that he had a drinking problem."

"He was an alcoholic?"

"That's not what I called it at the time. His drinking never interfered with his job, so I rationalized it wasn't so bad. He just liked to drink hard when he was off, and once he started, he wouldn't stop. He was never mean or violent when he drank. He just wasn't there—he was off in some other world where Riley and I didn't matter."

"Did you say anything to him about his drinking?"

"Oh yes. We had some spectacular fights. He always made the excuse that he worked a stressful job and was entitled to a release. And then he'd promise to cut back and we'd kiss and make up. For a while, things would be better."

"So you stayed with him."

"When he wasn't drinking, Pete was a great guy. A terrific father. Riley adored him. And I loved him. When you love someone, you forgive their shortcomings. I thought if I stuck with him, we could work it out."

"I hoped Melissa and I could overcome our problems, too, but she didn't share that hope."

"In the end I think I did overlook too much."

"Why do you say that?"

She hesitated, then said, "Pete always promised me he'd never drink too much when he was alone with Riley. I suspected that wasn't always the case, but I pretended it was. I couldn't believe he would ever do anything to endanger his son."

"My God—the accident?"

"Pete had been drinking that evening. He lost control of the car on an icy road. It rolled down an embankment and he and Riley were both killed. No other cars were involved, but a man saw them go over the edge and reported it."

Mike shuddered. He could picture the scene, see the bodies, as he'd seen so many others when he'd worked a rotation in the emergency room during his training. "Where were you that night?"

"Dancing at a private party."

She'd left her son with a man she knew might not stay sober—to go work. On the surface it was such a damning statement, as damning as "he was a doctor and never realized his own daughter was sick."

"It was my job," she said. "I'd made a commitment and needed to keep it. But I've never stopped feeling guilty about it, asking myself, what if I'd stayed home that night?"

"I'm surprised you didn't give up dancing."

"I thought about it, but it's what kept me sane. Through the worst of it, I could turn on the music and dance and forget, at least for the space of one song. Without that refuge, I think I would have lost my mind."

"I've always wondered how someone survives a tragedy like that," he said.

"I think part of me died with them that night. The part that trusted easily and believed everything always works out. But I didn't want to become a sad, bitter woman who lives in the past. Life goes on and I have to move forward, too. To do otherwise feels like it would be dishonoring their memories, somehow."

"You're remarkable," he said.

She shook her head. "The grief has a way of ambushing me. I'll be fine one minute, then something will happen and it's like it's brand-new all over again."

"Like the picture of Taylor in the hospital."

She nodded and blinked rapidly, her eyes shining.

He slid his hand across the table and twined his fingers with hers. She gripped him tightly, holding on, and again he felt the pull of attraction.

He wanted to comfort her—to make love to her and, in doing so, to comfort himself. He wanted to protect her, and to protect himself and Taylor from the kind of tragedy Darcy had suffered. She'd lost everything, and he had come to the very brink of the pit she was climbing out of.

Being with her forced him to face the reality that he only imagined he was in control of his life. She proved he wasn't. The idea repelled him and made him want to turn away.

But the woman herself compelled him to stay, the tension between them winding ever tighter, until all he could do was hold his breath and wait to see what the next words—or the next kiss—would bring.

CHAPTER SIX

ONE KISS DID NOT a relationship make. Darcy reminded herself of this whenever she thought of Mike during the next week. Granted, it had been a spectacular kiss and the memory of it left her feverish. But nice as it had been, she regretted she'd let down her guard so much. Mike was a great guy, but she'd never intended to reveal so much about her marriage—and her role in Riley's death—to him.

"What's up with you?" Jane asked Tuesday night, when Darcy flubbed a move in the dance she was teaching Jane's class. "You seem distracted."

"I just have a lot on my mind." Darcy glanced at the clock. "I think we've worked enough for one night, ladies. Keep practicing at home. Only four weeks until our show."

Jane lingered after the others left. "Hannah says the girls' class is going really well. She can't wait for Wednesdays and she's driving me crazy, changing her mind about her costume every five minutes."

"Hannah's really patient with the younger girls."

Jane beamed at this praise for her daughter. "I'm glad you started the class. You obviously really enjoy it. You look…I don't know, *happier*, lately," Jane said. "I thought maybe you'd met someone."

Darcy silently cursed her tendency to blush so easily. Mike was *someone*, all right, but how to explain her relationship with him when she didn't know how to define it? Mike was a friend, who knew things about her no one else did. But since when did she kiss a friend the way they'd kissed the other night? And since when did a mere friend punch out a guy for getting a little overenthusiastic about her dancing?

She still couldn't believe Mike hit that guy. It seemed so unlike the quiet, reserved doctor. Mike obviously had hidden emotional depths—depths she'd glimpsed again when he'd kissed her so passionately.

"I'm not dating anyone, if that's what you mean," she said.

"The offer's still open to introduce you to Eric's friend."

Darcy debated taking Jane up on it. It might be good for her to date someone. Someone without children. Going out with someone didn't mean she had to make a commitment to them, right? "I'll think about it."

She missed the days when she was young and her first thought at the promise of romance was of all the good times that lay ahead. Too much had happened to allow her to be that innocent again. Love could make a person happy beyond belief, and losing that loved one could damage her forever.

That's what Darcy was really afraid of, that she was too damaged to love again, that her heart was too broken for anyone to put it back together.

BY WEDNESDAY Darcy was jittery with nerves, torn between wanting to see Mike again and determination to avoid him. She still hadn't decided what to do, when the phone rang just as the girls were finishing their class. "Darcy? It's Mike. I need to ask a favor."

"Sure, Mike. What do you need?" She was surprised by how calm she sounded.

"I'm tied up here at the office this afternoon. Could you keep Taylor until I can get away to pick her up?"

His words—so practical and businesslike, so focused on his daughter—brought Darcy back down to earth. Of course there was nothing between her and Mike. He wasn't presuming anything based on a single kiss. She had nothing to worry about.

"Of course I'll look after Taylor," she said. "I have a few errands to run, so why don't I bring her to you at your office?"

"Not the office. I've seen two flu cases this morning and have a possible third scheduled for this afternoon. I don't want her exposed."

"I can take her to your house, then."

"I'll have my neighbor come over and watch Taylor until I get home. She's done that for me before."

"I don't mind staying with her," she said. "I don't have any more classes this evening."

"Are you sure?"

"Positive."

"Thanks. Taylor would like that." He hesitated, then added, "I'll look forward to seeing you too."

As declarations went, it wasn't much, but it was enough to launch her back into giddy uncertainty. Which was silly. After all, it was only one kiss. She looked around the room for Taylor. "Your dad is busy at the office with a bunch of flu cases," she said. "So I'm going to take you home."

Taylor made a face. "Do I have to stay with Mrs. Winslow?"

"I'll stay with you."

"All right! Mrs. Winslow won't let me out of her sight for one second. I think she's afraid I'm going to drop dead of a heart attack in front of her. If I so much as cough, she panics and wants to call Dad."

Darcy sympathized with the skittish Mrs. Winslow. While she didn't fear an imminent heart attack, the knowledge that Taylor's health was vulnerable was daunting. "I'm glad we get to spend some more time together," Darcy said as they climbed into her car.

"I'm old enough to stay by myself," Taylor said. "I mean, it's only an hour or so."

"Not my call," Darcy said. Though she wouldn't blame Mike if he refused to leave Taylor alone until she was eighteen.

At Mike's house, Taylor unlocked the door and they trooped inside. "Want to see my dad's ties?" she asked. "He has some cool ones. I like to go through them and pick out ones for him to wear."

"I shouldn't be going through your dad's things," Darcy said. "He's entitled to his privacy. You wouldn't want strangers coming in and going through your belongings, would you?"

"You're not a stranger. Want to see my troll doll collection instead?"

"Troll dolls?" Darcy laughed. "They still make those?"

"Sure." Taylor led her into her room, to an alcove beside the bed lined with shelves. The shelves were filled with troll dolls, their wild hair in every color of the neon rainbow. "Someone at the hospital gave me one when I first got sick," Taylor said. "I loved it, so other people started bringing them to me."

Darcy picked up a pink-haired troll mama with a snaggletoothed troll baby.

"I used to spend a lot of time combing their hair and stuff." Taylor stroked a purple-haired troll. "But now I just look at them." She set aside the purple troll and picked up one with bright red hair, dressed in a kilt. "My mom brought me this one from Scotland."

"Did you have a good time with your mother last weekend?" Darcy asked.

"Yeah. It was okay." She replaced the troll on the shelf. "We went to the ice show on Friday and shopping on Saturday, then had pizza Saturday night."

"Sounds like a fun weekend," Taylor said.

"Yeah, but…" She worried her lower lip between her teeth and glanced at Darcy. "Being with her is more like hanging out with a friend than a mom."

Darcy hoped when Melissa and Taylor were alone that Melissa paid more attention to her daughter. Taylor was at the age where she still enjoyed listening to her mother's stories, but how long would that last if she wasn't able to confide in Melissa in turn? Still, Melissa managed to remain involved in her daughter's life despite her hectic schedule. It wasn't Darcy's place to judge her. "I'm sure your mother loves you very much."

"Oh, I know that," Taylor said. "And I love her, too, and I like seeing her, but sometimes I wish she was more like a real mom."

"What do you mean?"

"I wish she did stuff like volunteering at my school and cooking dinner and things like that."

Darcy had done that kind of "stuff" for Riley. She'd helped in the school library and chaperoned field trips and brought refreshments to baseball practice. She'd made dinner most nights, even if it was only heated-up chicken nuggets and macaroni and cheese—his favorite.

"I almost forgot! I got a cool new computer game to show you." Taylor raced to the desk in the corner.

Darcy forced a smile, determined to set aside her sadness and focus on the child in front of her.

By the time Mike came home, Darcy had learned the ins and outs of a computer game involving dragons, princesses, handsome warriors and, yes, trolls, and was determined to survive at least one onscreen battle without going up in flames. She was so engrossed she didn't even notice Mike until he was standing behind her. "I see Taylor's introduced you to her latest obsession," he said.

His hand rested on the back of her chair, his fingers just grazing her shoulder. That casual contact sent a jolt of awareness through her. "Yes, I…yes, we were having fun," she stammered. "I'm afraid I'm not very good at it. She's beat me every round, but she's gracious enough to let me try again."

Stop babbling. She shut her mouth and stood. "I guess I'd better get going now."

"I at least owe you dinner for looking after Taylor this afternoon."

"Dinner? Oh, I don't know…" Dinner was too much like a date. The thought of being able to eat anything with her stomach fluttering so wildly was almost laughable.

"Please." He took her hand. "Taylor would enjoy it and I know I would."

His tone was warm and reassuring, his touch calming, spreading a pleasant heat through her. If this was an example of his bedside manner, it was a wonder he didn't have women lined up for blocks, waiting to see him.

This wouldn't be a date, really. Not with Taylor along. "All right," she said. "I'd love to have dinner with you."

The restaurant he chose was a small bistro near his home, with blue-and-white tablecloths and murals of the French countryside. The adults ordered steak and Taylor opted for chicken strips. Darcy's earlier nervousness had subsided, replaced by a pleasant buzz of energy. She thought Mike must have felt it, too. He smiled at her often and took every chance to touch her, fingers lightly brushing her hand as he passed the salt or poured wine. Taylor chattered away, seemingly oblivious.

They had just settled down to their meal when the door opened and Dave and Carrie came in.

"Darcy!" Dave quickly masked his surprise and strode to their table.

"Dave, this is Mike and Taylor Carter. Mike is a doctor. This is my brother, Dave." Darcy made the introductions. "Taylor is one of my students," she added. Maybe later she'd tell Dave about Taylor's heart, but not now. "And this is Dave's girlfriend, Carrie Kinkaid."

"Nice to meet you." The men shook hands, sizing each other up the way men do. Darcy wondered what her motorcycle-riding, construction-worker brother thought of the doctor. Mike had taken off his tie, but he still wore gray suit trousers and a blue-and-white pin-striped shirt. The top button of the shirt was unfastened and he'd rolled the sleeves to just below his elbows. Darcy kept staring at the fine dark hairs on his forearms and his thick, masculine fingers.

"How are you, Carrie?" Darcy asked.

"I'm good," Carrie said. "We've been looking at houses."

"*She's* been looking," Dave said. "I'm just the chauffeur. I like my place."

Carrie's mouth tightened. "Now's a great time to buy a house," Carrie said. "It would be a good investment."

"Yeah, all those people who've invested in real estate are really rolling in it now, considering how housing prices are down," Dave said.

"Which makes it a buyer's market," Carrie countered. "And prices will come back up."

"I don't think they're going anywhere right now," Dave said. "We've got plenty of time."

"I'm not so sure we do," Carrie said.

She had the uncomfortable feeling Carrie wasn't talking about the house. Darcy wondered what it was that kept Dave from marrying Carrie and settling down. After five years together, what was he waiting for?

"We'd better get out of here and let you eat," Dave said. "Nice to meet you, Mike. You, too, Taylor."

The hostess seated Dave and Carrie at a table across the room. Carrie said something to Dave and he scowled and shook his head.

"Are they going to get married?" Taylor asked.

The question surprised a gasp from Darcy. "Why would you think that?"

Taylor shrugged. "You said they were boyfriend and girlfriend, and they're buying a house. I mean, I know sometimes people just live together, but a marriage is more romantic, don't you think?"

"Some people would argue that marriage isn't always romantic," Mike said. But his eyes glinted with humor.

"Some parts of marriage certainly aren't romantic," Darcy agreed. There had been nothing romantic about her fights with Pete, and something much deeper and more enduring about their making up. She had many regrets about their relationship, and would always believe she should have done more to protect Riley. But she'd never regret the real love she and Pete had known when times were good.

"Are they going to get married?" Taylor asked.

"Taylor, that's none of your business," Mike chided.

"It's okay," Darcy said. "I don't know if Carrie and Dave will marry. They've been together a long time, and she'd like to get married, but he's not sure."

"It can be a scary proposition, to make that kind of commitment to another person," Mike said. "Especially when you've been on your own awhile."

Was he speaking from his own experience, or merely making conversation?

"If he loves her, I think they should get married," Taylor said.

Darcy nodded. The strength of her conviction surprised her. After all she'd been through with Pete and Riley, she would have said she never wanted to risk that pain again.

Of course, they were talking about Dave and Carrie. It was high time her brother got over his fear of commitment or belief in family curses or whatever was holding him back and settled down to raise the family he claimed he wanted.

She glanced toward the table where Dave and Carrie sat silently across from each other. Her heart ached to see two people she loved at such odds.

"When Taylor's mother and I bought our house, we had a hard time agreeing on a place," Mike said. "She wanted to be near the airport. I wanted to be close to my office."

"Your house is nowhere near the airport."

"Only because the schools on this side of town are better," he said. "And Melissa liked being by the lake. But it took us a while to get to that compromise. Maybe your brother and his girlfriend will find their perfect place, too."

Darcy had had a perfect place once, with a husband and son she loved. Losing them had destroyed her belief in perfection. Now she only wanted peace—a calm, Zen existence with dance and music and meditation, and no anger or fear or pain or any of those messy emotions that made life so hard.

Her eyes met Mike's and she knew he understood. They were after the same thing, really.

Which made the kiss they'd shared, and this attraction between them, a very scary thing. Being with someone else meant giving up some of that hard-won control. Taking risks.

Darcy liked Mike. And she adored Taylor. But she wasn't sure that was enough to move her past her fear of loving someone only to lose them.

As they ate, Mike studied Darcy, the way a fisherman studied the surface of a pond for a clue to what lay beneath. He still wasn't sure where he stood with her, or where he even wanted to stand. She intrigued him and awakened a side of him he'd ignored too long. Since his divorce he'd been content to remain single and celibate, but Darcy raised doubts. Maybe he wasn't as settled as he'd thought.

But if he was going to tiptoe back into the whole dating game, wouldn't it make more sense to start with someone less emotionally complicated than Darcy? Someone who didn't remind him so much of how fragile relationships could be?

"What do you have planned this weekend?"

At first Mike thought Darcy was addressing him, then he realized she was talking to Taylor.

"I don't know," Taylor said. "My mom is in Italy or Greece or someplace."

"Melissa's on a European rotation for the next month," Mike explained.

"Dad and I will probably just hang out at the house," Taylor said. "Do you want to hang out with us?"

Darcy shook her head, perhaps a little too forcefully. "I'm dancing at a birthday party on Saturday, and Friday night I have my regular gig at the restaurant."

"Do you do that every Friday?" Taylor asked.

"Starting next month it's only every other week."

"That's not because of what happened the other night, is it?" Mike asked, alarmed.

"Oh no. It's a slow time of year. We planned this before, I promise."

"I'll admit I'm relieved to hear it." He still couldn't believe he'd hit that guy—it was so unlike him. Then again, he didn't always feel like himself when he was with Darcy, though he couldn't yet say if that was good or bad.

"What are you talking about?" Taylor asked.

"Nothing, sweetheart."

The girl looked unconvinced. "You always say that when it's really something."

"I do not," Mike said.

"Yes you do. You always said that when you and Mom were fighting."

Mike made a face, and opened his mouth to launch into an explanation but Darcy cut him off. "Did Taylor tell you about the routine we've been learning in class?"

He shot her a look of gratitude. "No, she didn't. She won't even dance for me at home."

"I'm not good enough yet."

"You're doing very well in class," Darcy said. "All of you are."

"But I want to dance the way you do," she said.

"I've been dancing for ten years," she said. "I didn't start out being able to do all the moves I can do."

Mike couldn't keep from thinking about all those moves.

"You'll see her dance at my recital in a few weeks," Darcy said.

"I'm looking forward to it."

"Why can't you ever think about someone besides yourself and how *you* feel?"

The words were loud and anguished, coming from the table across the room where Darcy's brother and his girlfriend sat. The girlfriend—Carrie—shoved back her chair and stood. "You don't want me to leave so you won't have to be alone, but you don't want to be with me enough to make it permanent. Well, you can't have it both ways." She rushed past them, her face contorted by tears.

Darcy half rose from her chair, as if to follow, but her brother stopped her. "Stay out of this, sis," he said, and hurried after Carrie.

Darcy bit her lip, clearly distressed, but stayed in her seat. She glanced at Mike. "Sorry about that."

"What's wrong?" Taylor asked. "Why are they fighting?"

"I don't know," Darcy said. She smoothed her napkin across her lap once more. "It's none of my business, I guess. But he's the only family I have close by and I worry about him."

"Do you have other brothers and sisters?" Mike asked.

"No, it's just me and Dave. Mom's in Arizona now and Dad's in Las Vegas. They don't travel much anymore."

He imagined her after the accident, with only her brother to comfort her. "My parents are in Dallas," he said. He should visit them soon, and take Taylor. She needed to know her family better.

"Maybe your brother and his girlfriend will kiss and make up," Taylor said. "Or maybe they'll break up and he'll find someone new who will make him happier."

Mike stared at his daughter. Where had she gotten this cavalier attitude about romance? Was it because she'd witnessed the breakup of her parents' marriage? Or was it because he let her watch too much TV?

"I guess sometimes it's hard to know when you've found the right person," Darcy said. "I just want him to be happy. And Carrie's a nice person. I want her to be happy, too."

"Do you think it's like in stories, like Cinderella and Snow White—where there's one right person you're meant to fall in love with?" Taylor asked. "Or do you fall in love with lots of people in your lifetime?"

"Taylor, where do you get these ideas?" Mike asked. And why was she asking these questions now?

She shrugged. "Mom told me once, when we were talking about why you two got divorced, that people fell in love sometimes, and then as they got older and changed, that person wasn't right for them anymore and they had to split up so they'd be free to find the next right person."

Was that how Melissa saw it? Or was it simply easier to say that to a little girl who was wondering why her parents didn't love each other anymore? He had loved Melissa once, but he couldn't say she'd ever really been the right person for him—how could she be when they were so different?

"I think some people get lucky and find the one person they're meant to be with right away," Darcy said. "And other people have to look longer."

He thought of her husband, the alcoholic. If he'd lived, would they be divorced now?

"What about you?" Darcy asked Taylor. "Is there a boy at school you like?"

Once again she'd effectively steered the conversation away from personal revelations, though not exactly into territory Mike wanted to explore.

"There's this one guy in my class," Taylor said. "Nathan Orosco. He's really cute and, once, when I had to go in the hospital for some tests, he told me he was sorry I'd been sick."

"You're too young to be concerned with boys," Mike said.

"Lots of girls my age have boys they like," Taylor said.

"He's just being a dad," Darcy said. She looked as if she was trying not to laugh.

He forced himself to relax. "Nothing wrong with watching out for my daughter."

Taylor turned to Darcy. "I guess it's kind of cute, when you think about it."

"Yeah, it's cute," she said. Their eyes met and again he felt the pull of attraction. Darcy was definitely shaking up his life.

Being with her changed him—into a man who punched a stranger, who kissed a woman he barely knew. He didn't like losing control like that. Taylor and his patients depended on him to be steady and reliable. Getting close to a woman who made him lose it that way was out of the question.

CHAPTER SEVEN

THOUGH THE STUDENT RECITAL was still weeks away, the girls in Darcy's Wednesday afternoon class were engrossed in planning their favorite part of the event—their costumes. "I'm going to wear this sparkly top with all these sequins and fringe," Hannah said as they gathered in the studio before class.

"My mom made me this pink silky skirt and a matching short top," Zoe said. "It looks like something out of Aladdin."

"I have these velvet pants and this bra top with jewels on it," Debby said. She turned to Taylor. "What are you going to wear?"

"I don't know yet." Taylor busied herself zipping and unzipping her backpack. "It's still a long way off, anyway."

Darcy eavesdropped on their conversation from her spot by the stereo in the corner. She wished she could do something to ease Taylor's fears about her dance costume. Whatever scars she had from the surgery, they weren't important to those who loved her. She put a comforting hand on the girl's shoulder. "Why don't we call your father and ask if you can stay here after class today?" she said. "We can work on your costume."

Taylor looked doubtful. "Do you really think we can come up with something that won't look stupid?" she asked. "Maybe I shouldn't even dance."

Darcy ached for the girl. She wanted to pull her close and hold her tight, to reassure her the way a mother would.

But she wasn't Taylor's mother, only her teacher and friend. She couldn't take away the girl's pain, but she would find a way to make it not matter as much. "We'll come up with a great costume for you," she said. "Go ahead and call your father."

Taylor made the call and took her place in the lineup, her expression more relaxed.

After class, Darcy led Taylor to the spare bedroom that doubled as her sewing room. "I make a lot of my own costumes and I have material left over." She opened the closet and began pulling out plastic storage boxes stuffed with fabric and trim. "I'll bet we can find something in here to make you a costume."

Taylor popped the lid on the first box and fingered a swath of blue, shimmery organza. "This fabric is so gorgeous," she said.

"And it looks gorgeous on you." Darcy returned to the closet and pulled out a skirt made of panels of the blue organdy over purple satin. She'd made the costume to dance at a friend's wedding a few years back and it was still one of her favorites.

"Purple!" Taylor cried. "I want a purple costume."

Darcy laughed, relieved to see the girl so excited. "I think there's some purple in one of the other boxes."

They found what was left of the purple fabric, along with a flesh-colored thin knit. "You told me you like to watch ice-skaters, right?"

Taylor nodded. "They're my favorite in the Olympics. Dad always wants to watch ski jumping or racing, but I watch all the skaters."

"You know how their costumes sometimes have cutout areas where it looks like bare skin but it's really not? It's fabric like this. Dancers use this kind of fabric, too. We can use it for part of your costume so that from a distance it looks like your skin."

Taylor stared up at her. "Do they really do that?"

"All the time. Some of my older students aren't comfortable showing their stomachs, so they cover up, but on stage they look like everyone else."

"That's what I want," Taylor said. "To look like everyone else."

"You'll look even better," Darcy promised. "Now stand up so I can measure you."

As Darcy stretched the tape measure across her chest, Taylor sighed. "Because I was sick and then had the transplant, and now I take all this medicine,

I'm behind everything for my age," she said. "Dad says I'll catch up, but he doesn't say when. My friend, Keisha, already has her period, and a lot of the girls at school wear training bras."

Taylor showed no signs of needing a bra of any kind. Her body was still that of a child, though in many other ways she was mature beyond her years. "Everyone develops at a different rate. I was always what my mother called a late bloomer."

"What does that mean?" Taylor asked.

"It means I didn't develop much of a figure until I was out of high school. Honestly, I was flat as a pancake up top until I had Riley."

"I think about him a lot, you know." Taylor put one hand over her heart. "Even before I met you. I always wondered what he was like. The Donor Alliance told me my heart came from a boy, and I know that's not really supposed to make any difference, but I always wondered…"

"I can tell you he wouldn't have been interested in doing this." Darcy recorded the measurement in a notebook. "He was typical boy, into sports and cars." As much as she loved her son, he'd been so different from her, and she'd known the differences would only mount as he grew older.

But of course, he'd never grown older. To her he would always be six. "I always secretly wanted a girl I could do stuff with," she said. "Not instead of Riley, but as a sister for him."

"Why didn't you have another kid?" Taylor asked. "Or is that one of those questions my dad says I shouldn't ask?"

"I don't mind answering. I wanted another baby, but my husband thought we should wait." She hesitated, wondering how much was appropriate to tell a young girl. "Pete was a good father to Riley, but he had a drinking problem. I worried it wasn't right to bring another child into that situation."

"Did it bother Riley that his father drank?"

"It did sometimes." She had occasionally wondered what would have happened if Riley and Pete had survived the accident. But no good came of speculation. "I'm thinking we can do a skirt like mine," she said. "And then a short top, with lots of sequins and beads, and a matching hip belt, and the body stocking fabric underneath."

"Can I help make it?"

"Of course you can. Let's start by drawing up a pattern."

She sketched the design on tissue paper, then let Taylor color in the drawing while she cut the pattern pieces out of more tissue paper. "Will you show me how to operate the sewing machine?" Taylor asked.

"Sure," Darcy said. "You can help put on the sequins, too."

"I like crafts," Taylor said. "Mom doesn't do them. She said she'd rather buy whatever she wants."

"I like to shop, too," Darcy said. "But sometimes it's fun to be more creative."

"Maybe I'll be a fashion designer when I grow up," Taylor said. "Only instead of regular clothes, I'll design special ones—stuff that will look pretty but hide surgery scars, or scars from people who've been burned, and things like shirts that are easy to take on and off, for people who are missing an arm."

"That's an excellent idea." She could picture Taylor, grown into a beautiful young woman, in charge of her own successful business. The strength of her desire to continue to be a part of Taylor's life, to know what happened to her, stunned Darcy. It was the same sort of longing she'd had for a baby before she conceived Riley.

On the heels of this longing came a surge of joy. Though Taylor's future health concerned Darcy, she hoped this ability to contemplate being a part of someone else's life again was a sign that the worst of her grief had passed.

Two hours later, they had cut out all the pieces of the costume and sewn a couple of seams on the skirt when Mike arrived. "Dad, look what I did. I sewed this myself," Taylor announced, running to him with the unfinished skirt billowing behind her like a flag.

"That's great, honey." Mike admired the somewhat crooked seams, then smiled at Darcy. "Looks like the costume's coming together well."

"It's going to be fabulous," Taylor said.

"We'll work on it more next week," Darcy said. "That is, if it's okay with your dad."

"Fine with me," Mike said. "If you're sure it's not imposing on your time."

Their eyes met and Darcy felt the thrill of attraction. Forget cooking—the way to this man's heart was through his daughter.

Mike was the first to look away. "We'd better not keep you any longer," he said. "Taylor, get your things so we can go."

Taylor raced back to the sewing room, where she'd left her backpack. Darcy seized the opportunity to pull Mike into her laundry room.

"What are you doing?" he protested.

"This." She wrapped her arms around him and kissed him soundly, as if her life—or at least her future—depended on it.

THE KISS WAS the kind men—or at least Mike—fantasized about, all heat and passion and intensity, erasing all the rationalizing and analyzing and thinking that was so much a part of his life, touching some primitive animal instinct.

He pulled Darcy more tightly against him, deepening the kiss, claiming her with his mouth as one hand slid down to cup the roundness of her bottom and the other slanted across her shoulders. She let out a soft moan and he pressed her back against the washing machine, the silk of her shirt sliding against his hand as he shifted position, one thigh thrust between her legs.

"Dad, I—oops!"

The small voice jerked him out of a haze of lust. Still clinging to Darcy, he looked over his shoulder. Taylor stood in the doorway, one hand to her mouth, not quite covering her grin.

"Sorry, Taylor. We didn't mean to embarrass you." Darcy's voice was shaky as she extricated herself from Mike's grasp. He stepped back and shoved his hands in his pockets, his face burning. He stared at the floor, at the washing machine—anywhere but at his daughter or Darcy.

"It's not like I've never seen people kissing before." She giggled. "But not Dad. At least not since I was little, and then just Mom and he never kissed her that way—"

"We'd better go now." Mike gripped Taylor's shoulder and turned her toward the kitchen, and the exit.

"See you soon," Darcy said.

He risked a glance at her. Her cheeks were flushed, her hair mussed, and her lips were slightly swollen. She looked like a woman who'd just had sex, and the thought made him hard all over again.

One thing she didn't look was the least bit ashamed or embarrassed at being caught by his ten-year-old daughter. Not that they'd been doing anything wrong, exactly, but it certainly wasn't like him to act so impulsively.

In the car on the way home, he chose his words carefully. "I don't want you to get the wrong idea about Darcy and me."

"I'm glad you like her," Taylor said. "I like her too. I think she'd make a cool stepmom."

"Stepmom?" His heart pounded. "Taylor, Darcy and I hardly know each other." Not that he wanted his daughter to think it was okay to go around kissing virtual strangers. "We're friends. That's all."

"You weren't kissing her like a friend."

"What would you know about that?"

"Dad—I watch TV."

Obviously, he needed to pay more attention to what she was watching.

"I think it's cool if you have a girlfriend," Taylor said. "Sometimes I feel guilty that you don't, like maybe it's my fault."

"The fact that I don't have a girlfriend has nothing to do with you," he said. That wasn't entirely true. Without Taylor in his life, he might be with someone. Or he might not. He wasn't the swinging-bachelor type. His medical practice claimed a lot of his time and what was left he devoted to Taylor.

He glanced in the rearview mirror. Taylor was watching him, a serious look on her face. "Do you want a stepmother, is that it?" he asked. At ten, on the brink of so many changes in her body and in her life, Taylor probably felt the absence of a woman more keenly than at any time since he and Melissa had divorced.

She shrugged. "I don't need a stepmom, I just wanted you to know I'm okay with it if you want to marry again. As long as it's someone nice."

"And you think Darcy is nice."

"Yeah. And you must think she's nice, too, or you wouldn't have kissed her that way." She giggled again.

That way. Like a randy teenager who couldn't control his emotions.

Or a man who'd been alone too long. "I have no plans to marry Darcy, or anyone else right now," he said. "When I do, you'll be the first to know."

"You should probably tell the woman first."

He shook his head and tried to focus on his driving. But all he could think of was Darcy—the way she tasted and felt. The way she smelled. The look in her eyes when they'd parted. It was full of mischief and passion and delight, as if she knew exactly how much he wanted her and was very pleased with the idea.

It was an idea that ought to please him, too.

Yes, he wanted Darcy, in the physical sense. Darcy was alive and passionate, glowing with an inner light he envied. She had been through more than any one person should have to bear, yet she hadn't lost herself to suffering. His own losses seemed trivial in comparison, and yet he felt as if he'd been permanently affected by them.

Whatever his feelings for Darcy, he couldn't call any of them love. Love was something that grew over time. It didn't ambush a man the way his desire for Darcy had taken him in her laundry room just now. He had dated Melissa for two full years before he'd told her he loved her.

He'd been drawn to Melissa in part because she was so unlike him. At the time he'd told himself they filled in the gaps in each other's personality. Yet the marriage had been a disaster.

Now he was on the verge of making the same kind of mistake with Darcy, letting desire blind him to the differences between them. Had he learned nothing from the past?

"Dad, do you think one day I can have plastic surgery?"

"Plastic sur— Taylor, what are you talking about?" He slammed on the brakes at a stop sign and turned to stare at his daughter.

She stuck out her lower lip, glowering in a way that was so much like Melissa he didn't know whether to laugh or despair. "Darcy's making me a costume that covers up my scars, but I'll still look different from all the other girls. It would be so much better if I could just have plastic surgery to make them go away."

The guy in the car behind them honked and Mike resisted the urge to make an obscene gesture. He faced forward and started driving again, trying to gather his thoughts. "We've talked about this before," he said. "The scars will fade over time. They're already much less noticeable to other people than they are to you." Every one of those scars was precious to him, a reminder of the miracle that had saved her.

"Darcy says there's special makeup made to cover scars like mine. She said maybe we could go shopping for some."

Darcy again. She claimed to be teaching the girls to accept their bodies, so what was she doing discussing makeup with a ten-year-old? "I don't think you need to be wearing makeup."

"But Darcy said—"

"I'm your father and I say no." He cringed, waiting for Taylor's face to crumple into tears, but she only continued to glower, her silence like a cold knife slicing him.

He gripped the steering wheel until his knuckles throbbed. This was partly his fault. He'd let a woman's attractive figure and a passionate kiss distract him from his responsibilities to his daughter.

Yes, Darcy had made the generous decision to donate her son's heart so that Taylor could live. Yes, Taylor liked her, but what girl wouldn't? She was pretty and fun and she didn't have a clue how fragile Taylor really was.

Now she'd gone too far, upsetting Taylor with all

this talk about her scar, when Mike was sure they'd been past all that.

Maybe Darcy was even the one who'd brought up the stepmom idea. Maybe she looked at his house and his medical practice and saw an opportunity to move up in the world.

He felt sick to his stomach. Darcy wasn't like that.

But how did he really know? They'd shared a couple of meals, a cup of coffee and two intense kisses. He couldn't claim to have been thinking clearly through any of that, distracted as he was by lust.

He glanced in the mirror at Taylor again. Her head was turned and she was looking out the side window. His first job was to protect her. He couldn't let one woman, no matter how seemingly well-meaning, take over their lives.

All the passion in the world wasn't worth upsetting his daughter.

CHAPTER EIGHT

DARCY TOLD HERSELF she had no reason to regret her impulsiveness in kissing Mike, but his car was scarcely out of the driveway before doubts assailed her. It was one thing to enjoy Mike's lips on hers and his arms around her, but she shouldn't have let Taylor see them together like that.

After all, Mike had made it very clear that night in the coffee shop that he wasn't interested. And Darcy couldn't pretend she was ready for a serious relationship. She'd acted impulsively, living in the moment, something she hadn't done much of since Riley's and Pete's deaths. It felt almost too good to let go of the reserve she'd built up as a kind of wall around her emotions. She still needed to protect herself.

She tried to call Dave. Talking to her brother about his problems would distract her from her own. But Dave didn't answer his phone. Maybe he and Carrie were kissing and making up, as Taylor had suggested.

But when he didn't answer again when she phoned the next morning, she drove to his condo, trying not to imagine the worst. She rang the bell, then knocked, and was debating calling the police when the door finally opened. His shirt was untucked and he needed a shave…he looked perfectly normal.

"What took you so long?" she asked, pushing past him into the living room. "I was starting to worry."

"I was in the basement."

"I tried calling this morning. And last night. You never answered."

"I didn't feel like talking." He headed down the stairs. She followed at his heels, surprised by the thinning patch of hair at the back of his head. When had Dave begun losing his hair?

"Where's Carrie?" she asked.

"I don't know."

"What do you mean you don't know?"

"She left."

Darcy's spirits sank. "Oh, Dave. Why? Is this about the house?"

"Mind your own business, sis."

Most of the basement had been converted into a woodworking shop. A workbench filled one end of the room, with bins of lumber and projects in various stages of completion crowded between the water heater and the washing machine. The air smelled of wood shavings and varnish.

Dave headed for the workbench and picked up a length of wood—a chair spindle, she guessed.

"What did you say to Carrie in the restaurant the other night?" she asked.

"Stay out of it." He shoved a pair of safety glasses over his eyes, then switched on a lathe.

Darcy watched him work, not put off for a minute by his gruff manner. Dave hadn't listened to her when she'd tried to get him to leave her alone after Riley and Pete had died. He'd stayed right with her, making her soup and handing her tissues and refusing to let her wallow in her despair.

Maybe this thing between him and Carrie wasn't her business, but she wouldn't leave him to suffer alone. He might think he didn't want to talk about it, but she'd be here if he did.

He shut off the lathe and picked up a piece of sandpaper and began rubbing down the wood. "What are you making?" Darcy asked.

"A rocking chair." He inspected the piece and resumed sanding. "It's a commission."

"That's terrific!" His ambition was to open a shop making custom furniture. Construction work was what he did to fill in the gaps while he built his business. "Who's it for?"

"That new birthing center at the women's hospital. If they like this one, they'll order more." His eyes met hers, excitement shining in them.

"That's wonderful. Congratulations." Carrie must be so proud. So why wasn't she here?

He returned to his sanding. "I told Car this wasn't a good time to buy a house, that I was saving for a shop."

"Why not buy a house with a garage you could use as a shop?"

"That's not what I want."

And of course it was all about what *he* wanted. Poor Carrie. Now that she'd pushed him, Dave was never going to back down.

"What's with you and that doctor?" Dave asked.

"Mike?" She trailed one hand along the edge of the bench, deliberately casual. "I told you, his daughter is in one of my classes."

"So where's the girl's mother?"

"They're divorced."

"You two dating?"

"Not exactly." They'd only spent a few hours together without Taylor around. He'd punched a guy on her behalf. They'd enjoyed two incredible kisses. But what did all that add up to?

"What are you doing with a guy like that? I thought you'd have had your fill of doctors after all they put you through."

He meant after Pete and Riley died. She'd battled with doctors and the hospital and the insurance company for a full year after the funerals, every new bill or statement ripping the wounds open again. "Mike's a nice guy," she said.

"Cute kid." He set aside the spindle and picked up another one and began sanding it.

"Taylor's great." She hesitated, then said, "We met because of her."

"You already said that. She's in your class."

"Yes, but there's more to it than that. She...she has Riley's heart."

He froze, gripping the spindle. A piece of sandpaper fluttered to the floor. "I didn't think you were supposed to meet donor recipients."

"We found out by accident. One of life's weird coincidences."

"I don't know. Do you really think getting friendly with these people is a good idea?"

"Why wouldn't it be?"

"I'm just saying, are you really interested in this guy, or just trying to replace what you lost?"

She gasped, and struggled to find her voice. "That's not what's going on. Just because I'm friends with Taylor and with her father doesn't mean I'm trying to replace Riley or Pete."

"Yeah, but this kid, you don't think to some degree you're looking for Riley in her?"

She wanted to deny him, to tell him he was crazy. The heart was just an organ. A body part that no more carried any trace of Riley's personality than his little finger would have.

But there was no sense lying to Dave, or to herself. "Of course I'm happy that a piece of him lives on in Taylor. But she's not my son. She's her own, distinct person."

His expression grew gentler. "I'd just hate to see

you hurt. And I really don't want to have to go to the trouble of kicking the guy's ass if he hurts you."

That surprised a laugh from her.

"What's so funny?" Dave asked.

She shook her head. "Nothing. It's just—" She laughed again. "You might be the one to come out on the losing end of that fight. A couple of weeks ago, Mike came to the restaurant where I was dancing. One of the customers had had too much to drink and Mike laid him out on the floor with one punch."

"No kidding? Good for him."

"Dave! I could have lost the job."

"Yeah, but if you marry the doctor, you won't need to work."

"Who said anything about marriage?"

"Are you sleeping with him?"

"No! We haven't even had dinner without his daughter there."

"If he's punching out guys in restaurants, he wants to sleep with you, whether he's done anything about it or not."

"Dave!" She felt her face flame, but she couldn't keep back a smile, either.

"We both know sleeping with someone doesn't mean marriage and happily ever after," she said. "You've been sleeping with Carrie for five years yet you won't ask her to marry you."

Dave scowled. "She pushes too hard. I don't like to be pushed."

"So you'd rather lose the woman who loves you than give in an inch?"

"If she loves me so much, why is she trying to change things between us? Why can't we go on the way we have been?"

"Because sometimes," she said, "we settle for the status quo because it's easy, not because it's right."

He resumed sanding the piece. "Don't quote self-help books to me. I like my life the way it is. If Carrie can't accept that, I won't make her stay."

Darcy swallowed her disappointment. Dave certainly didn't look heartbroken. Maybe she'd been wrong and he didn't love Carrie after all. If he loved her, he'd do anything to keep her, wouldn't he?

What did she know about love, anyway? She had loved Pete, but in the way some people love cigarettes or drugs or other things that bring them momentary pleasure but aren't really good for them. And Pete had loved to drink more than he loved her. It wasn't a conscious choice; it was just how he was wired. Knowing this hurt so much she hadn't been able to acknowledge it until long after he died.

Along with the loss of her husband and child, she mourned the death of their chance to ever have a healthy relationship, to ever love each other fully, as a man and a woman should.

Or at least as she thought they should. Maybe it was all fairy-tale thinking. She put her hand on Dave's shoulder. "I just want you to be happy," she said. "If Carrie isn't the woman you want to be with, then I hope you'll find the right person."

"I never said I didn't want to be with her. I just don't want her to try to shove me into some mold where I don't fit."

"So you want her, but only on your terms."

"What's wrong with that?"

"Nothing, except relationships require compromise—on both sides." When one person made all the sacrifices, as she had with Pete, the only thing that grew between them was resentment.

"There you go, talking like a self-help book again." He tossed the used sandpaper toward a trashcan. He missed, and it bounced across the floor and came to rest beside a pile of similar wadded papers.

"You're a lousy shot," she said.

"Go home, Darcy. Worry about your own life for a change."

Change was exactly what she needed. "Maybe I'll call Mike and ask if he wants to sleep with me."

"If that's what makes you happy. Maybe if you get laid you'll be too busy to stick your nose in my life."

"I'm never too busy for that." She started across the room, but paused to pick up one of the discarded wads of sandpaper and fire it at him.

It hit him in the back, and he waved at her without looking up. "Go."

"I'm going." Going to take his advice and live

her life. She probably wouldn't call Mike and openly proposition him, but she'd find a way to let him know she was interested—in sex or love or whatever he was offering.

She was tired of being afraid of the future, and ready to take a little risk, if Mike was willing to take the risk with her.

"SOUNDS LIKE you're doing much better today." Mike moved his stethoscope across Brent Jankowski's narrow chest and listened to the steady beat of his heart, and the rush of breath in and out of almost clear lungs. "I think that bronchitis is on its way out."

"I'm so glad to hear that," Sarah Jankowski said. She touched Brent's head, a brief gesture of reassurance Mike recognized. In the weeks after Taylor's transplant, he hadn't been able to stop touching her, to verify that she was really here.

He removed the stethoscope and stepped back. "Continue the antibiotic for another ten days. Are you using a humidifier in his bedroom at night?"

"Always. If I don't, he gets nosebleeds."

Mike nodded. "Keep it up, at least through the winter."

"Can I go outside during recess at school now?" Brent asked. "I'm tired of sitting in the library while everyone else gets to play."

"If you bundle up well and don't overdo it," Mike

said. "And don't hesitate to call if you have any problems."

"Thank you, Doctor. We will," Sarah Jankowski promised.

Mike was washing his hands when Peggy bustled into the room. "The school is on line one."

Telling himself there was no need to be too concerned, but heart racing all the same, he walked around the corner and picked up the phone there and punched the glowing button of line one. "This is Dr. Carter."

"This is the school nurse. I'm afraid you need to come get Taylor."

"What's wrong? Is she sick?"

"She's not sick, but she is hurt—though not badly. She's been in a fight."

"A fight?" His little girl? "Someone hit her?"

"From what I understand, she hit the boy first. Why don't you come on down here and we'll discuss it."

He hung up and headed for his office, feet moving automatically, his mind spinning. "I have to go get Taylor from school," he said as he passed the front desk, peeling off his lab coat as he walked. "Reschedule anyone you can. Apologize to everyone else."

"What's wrong?" Peggy called, but he was already out the back door to the parking lot.

At the school, the nurse, Mrs. Jenkins and the principal, Mr. Rouse, met Mike at the door to the office.

"Taylor is fine," Mr. Rouse reassured him. "Just a black eye and a few bruises."

"What happened?" he asked. "What's this about her hitting a boy?"

"They exchanged...words on the playground," Mr. Rouse said. "And she hit him. Things escalated from there until two teachers pulled them apart."

"How do you know she hit him first?" Mike asked, trying to wrap his mind around the picture of his daughter brawling in the schoolyard.

"We have several witnesses, including the two teachers."

"They saw what was happening and didn't stop it?"

"The last thing they expected was for your daughter to punch the boy."

"It was a good, solid hit," Mrs. Jenkins volunteered. "She split his lip."

"Where is she?"

Taylor sat on the exam table in the nurse's office, head down, feet dangling. One kneesock sagged, and there was a rip in the sleeve of her blouse. She looked up when they walked in, revealing a swollen left eye that was beginning to blacken. "Daddy!" she cried, and burst into noisy sobs.

He rushed over to her, cradling her head against his shoulder, handing her his handkerchief. "Calm down," he said. "It's all right."

One soggy handkerchief and a glass of water later,

she had calmed somewhat, though Mike was feeling more agitated by the minute. He examined the eye, which was swollen but not damaged. It probably hurt, though, and would turn all kinds of ugly colors before it healed. "Tell me what happened," he said.

Still clinging to him, she looked at Mr. Rouse and Mrs. Jenkins, who stood with arms crossed, waiting. "You have to tell us," Mike prompted.

"I was on the playground with Kira and Hannah, from my dance class. Some of the other girls wanted to see some moves, so we were showing them and Nathan walked by and said the others were pretty good, but I was too ugly to be a belly dancer. He made me so mad!"

Mike clenched his fists but forced himself to remain calm. They were talking about a boy here. "That's why you hit him?"

She nodded. "I didn't mean to. I didn't think about it or anything. I just wanted to stop his ugly grin."

"Taylor, you can't hit every person who says mean things to you."

"I know." She began to cry again, more quietly this time. "But he was wrong. He shouldn't have said something so mean."

Shaky with anger and frustration and helplessness, Mike looked at Mr. Rouse. "How's the boy?"

"He'll be fine. Though other boys will give him a hard time about getting beat up by a girl." The principal's expression sobered. "They're both suspended for three days. It's the automatic punishment for fighting."

Mike nodded. "I'll take Taylor home now."

On the ride to his office, Taylor was sullen. "I'll put something on that eye, then you'll have to stay at the office until I finish seeing my patients for the day," he said.

"Can't I stay with Darcy?"

His hands tightened on the steering wheel. If it weren't for Darcy and her belly dancing class, none of this would have happened. "Darcy has to work. We can't impose on her because you did something wrong."

"I said I was sorry."

"I know you are. But what you did was absolutely unacceptable. People are going to say hurtful things to you. That's life. You can't solve your problems with violence." He might have expected such behavior from a boy, but from a girl who still played with dolls and liked makeup and fancy shoes and all those feminine things? He shook his head.

At the clinic office, he was happy to turn her over to Peggy and Nicole, who clucked over her injured eye and commiserated about mean boys. Mike retreated to his office, where he donned his lab coat and stethoscope, but hesitated before returning to his patients. He picked up the phone and punched in Darcy's number.

"Hello?" She answered on the fifth ring, out of

breath. He pictured her in one of her skimpy outfits, cheeks flushed, hair mussed. The image was entirely too alluring.

"It's Mike," he said. "I didn't mean to interrupt."

"It's okay. What's up?"

"I'm calling to let you know Taylor won't be in class this week."

"Is she all right? She's not sick, is she?"

"No, she's not sick. But she's grounded. She got into a fight at school and was suspended for three days."

"A fight? Was she hurt?"

"She has a black eye. I think her feelings are hurt more than anything, though."

"What happened?"

He told her about the boy, and his remark that Taylor wasn't pretty enough to be a belly dancer.

"That's horrible! What was this boy's name?"

"Nate or Nathan something or other. I don't re-member."

"Nathan Orosco."

"Maybe. How did you know?"

"That's the boy in her class she said she liked. She told us at dinner the other night. Don't you remember?"

No. He had put the information right out of his mind because she was too young. "I don't think she likes him anymore," he said. "After he said that to her, she hauled off and hit him. Split his lip." If Mike was lucky, the boy's parents wouldn't sue.

"Good for her for standing up for herself."

"Darcy! She hit the boy. That's no way to act."

"No. And I don't approve of fighting, but sometimes when we have strong feelings about something we act without thinking."

He thought of the man he'd hit in the restaurant. He certainly hadn't been thinking that night. Was that kind of behavior hereditary? "You didn't tell Taylor about that night at the restaurant, did you?" he asked.

"Of course not. But it is a good example of how emotions can sometimes carry us away."

He'd let himself get carried away all right, his attraction to Darcy overriding common sense. "I'm not sure if Taylor should come back to your class."

"Why not? She loves dancing and she's doing so well."

"If it weren't for belly dancing, this never would have happened."

"That's ridiculous. Don't you remember how boys are?"

"We're not talking about the boy. We're talking about Taylor."

"This is about Taylor. That boy likes her, so he said the first thing he could think of to get her attention. It's classic male thinking."

"How do you know so much about it? You weren't a boy."

"No, but I did give birth to one. And he acted the same way. He once told a girl he liked that she looked like a frog."

"I still think it's not a good idea to encourage Taylor by letting her continue to take dance."

"And I think if it weren't for dance class she wouldn't have had the guts to stand up for herself. Yes, it was wrong for her to hit the boy. But do you remember how self-conscious she was about her looks when she first came to me? She still has a ways to go, but I'll bet a few weeks ago if a boy she liked had said something to her like that it would have crushed her. At least now some part of her is telling her he's wrong."

"I don't understand why she's so hung up on her looks," he said. "She's a beautiful girl—and I'm not just saying that because I'm her father."

"She *is* beautiful, but society puts a lot of pressure on girls—even Taylor's age—to look and act a certain way. Girls are always comparing themselves, seeing where they don't measure up."

"Melissa and I have been careful not to raise Taylor to think like that."

"That's great, but unless you hide her in a cave she's going to be exposed to it through television and movies and even at school. The best you can hope for is that other things—like my class—will offset that."

"I think your class makes her think about it even more. I mean look at you. You're gorgeous. Any girl is liable to feel intimidated by your looks."

He hadn't meant to say that, but then again, she must know how he felt about her, how most men probably felt about her.

"Thank you, but I don't think I'm the problem here. If you take this away from Taylor she'll hate you for it."

"Part of being a parent is having your children hate you for looking after their best interests."

"Mike, you're upset right now. I'm upset, too. Keep Taylor home this week if you think that's best, but please don't pull her out of class altogether."

"I'll think about it."

"Can I talk to Taylor?"

"Not right now. She's beginning to calm down and going through the story again would only upset her."

"Why don't you tell her to call me later, if she wants."

"All right."

"You can call me, too," she said. "You know, if you need to blow off steam."

"Or if I need any more insight into the male mind."

She laughed, that light, musical sound that pierced

him to the heart. He hung up, then sat for a long moment, staring at nothing. Maybe protecting Taylor wasn't the only reason he wanted to pull her out of Darcy's class. Discontinuing her dance lessons would make it easier for him to distance himself from Darcy, and from the intense feelings she kindled in him. It was too easy to forget himself when he was with her—to forget his responsibilities and obligations. Darcy made him feel good, but he wasn't sure she was good for him, or for Taylor.

She was right that Taylor had changed since meeting Darcy.

He just wasn't sure the change was for the best.

CHAPTER NINE

TAYLOR DIDN'T CALL DARCY, and neither did Mike. Darcy told herself they were too busy, or maybe part of Taylor's punishment was that she couldn't talk on the phone. And despite Mike's comment about her being gorgeous, she'd sensed a coolness in his voice when they'd spoken, as if he really did blame her for Taylor's fighting.

Wednesday, her girls' class could talk of nothing but the fight. "Taylor really socked Nathan good," Kira said. "Right on the mouth. He was bleeding and everything."

"He looked like he was going to cry," Hannah said. "I thought he would, but he punched Taylor instead."

"Then *she* started crying," Kira added.

Darcy winced. "I imagine her eye hurt." She wished she could have been there to comfort the girl after the boy she liked spoke so cruelly to her.

"I saw them taking her to the office," Debby said. "Her eye was all swollen and purple. It did look like it hurt."

"They're both suspended and can't come back to school until next week," Hannah said.

What was Taylor doing during her suspension? Was she staying with a babysitter, or stuck in Mike's office all day? Darcy would have gladly looked after the girl, if Mike had asked. But of course, he hadn't asked, one more sign that he blamed her for what had happened.

"I still can't believe Taylor hit him," Hannah said.

"It doesn't sound as if either one of them handled the situation well," Darcy said carefully.

"I'll bet he won't say mean things to her again," Debby said.

"Yes, but hitting people isn't a good way to solve problems," Darcy said. "What else could she have done?"

"She could have told a teacher he was being mean," Zoe said.

"She could have ignored him," Hannah suggested.

"She could have shown him a few more moves and proved she was a good dancer," Kira said.

Darcy doubted Taylor would have had the nerve to dance for a boy like that, but she admired Kira's attitude. "Those are all great suggestions," she said. "Maybe you'll remember them if anyone ever says ugly things to you. Now, speaking of good dancers, we've got a show to practice for."

As they moved on to the dance they were learning for the recital, Darcy felt Taylor's absence keenly. After the girls left, she took out the costume she'd been making for Taylor, thinking working on it would help her feel closer to the girl. But it only made Darcy miss her more.

Mike thought he knew how to handle this, but did he really? Men had such different attitudes than women when it came to things like this. She remembered when Riley was five. He'd been targeted by a bully at school, a bigger, older kid who pushed him around on the playground and took his lunch money.

Riley had grown sullen and silent at home, picking at his meals and not sleeping well. At first he'd refused to tell them what was wrong, but Darcy had pressed and finally the story came out. Darcy had vowed to go up to the school and confront the principal and Riley's teacher, but Pete had held her back.

"He needs to learn how to handle this on his own," he'd said.

"He's only five years old!" she'd protested. He'd have time enough later to learn to be a man. Now, he was still her baby.

She'd talked to the principal and to the teacher. They'd been defensive at first, but the bully was sent to counseling and Riley was happy again.

Clearly, there were some things a child needed her mother for. But Darcy wasn't Taylor's mother. And no matter what Dave said, she wasn't trying to make Taylor a substitute for Riley. Right now Taylor simply needed a woman who understood her and what she was going through.

Darcy put away her sewing and checked the clock. It was after seven, late enough Mike and Taylor would have finished supper but Taylor wouldn't be in bed yet.

She stopped at the grocery store on the way to Mike's house and bought flowers and a funny card she thought Taylor would like.

Mike was clearly surprised to see her. "Darcy! What are you doing here?"

"I came to see Taylor." She held up the bouquet of flowers. "I thought she might need cheering up."

He frowned. "She's supposed to be grounded."

"I understand. I'd still like to say hello and let her know we missed her in class today."

His frown didn't fade, but he stepped back and let her in. "She's in her room."

"How is she?" Darcy asked.

"I don't know. She won't talk to me."

Taylor sat in front of her computer, her back to Darcy, earbuds blocking her hearing as she played the video game with the princesses, dragons and trolls. "Taylor?" Darcy said.

The girl turned and Darcy choked back a gasp. Her left eye was ringed with purple and black, the lid swollen almost shut. "Your poor eye!"

"It doesn't hurt too much," Taylor said. "Dad says the worst will be over by the time I go back to school Monday. My suspension is up Friday, but that's a teacher's work day."

"I brought you these." Darcy held out the flowers and card.

"Thanks." Taylor took them and opened the card, smiling briefly. "I don't have anything to put these in," she said.

Darcy looked around and spotted a glass on the bedside table. It might have once held milk. She took it into the bathroom, rinsed it out and refilled it, then stuck the flowers in it. It was no professional arrangement, but it would do.

When Darcy returned to the bedroom, Taylor was sitting cross-legged on the bed. "I'm sorry I couldn't be in class today," she said.

"We missed you. We talked about nonviolent ways to respond when someone says mean things about us."

Taylor looked even sadder. "I know I shouldn't have hit him. And I said I was sorry."

"It was Nathan, wasn't it?" Darcy said. "The boy you like."

"I don't like him anymore. I never knew he was so mean."

Darcy sat on the edge of the bed. She wanted to pull Taylor close in a hug, but was afraid if she did so they'd both burst into tears. Not that a good cry wouldn't have been appropriate, but she didn't want Mike to come in and accuse her of upsetting his daughter. She wondered if he was listening outside the door. In his place, she might have been.

"Boys, especially boys that age, have a hard time showing a girl they like her," she said. "So they try to do things to get her attention—even mean things."

"He said I was ugly." Taylor bit her lip, blinking rapidly.

"This is going to sound weird," Darcy said. "But guys are weird sometimes. And I think—maybe— Nathan told you you were ugly because really, he thinks you're pretty."

"That's stupid."

"Yes. But people do stupid things sometimes. Fighting is stupid, too, don't you think?"

She nodded. "I won't do it again."

"You're a very pretty girl, Taylor. It's good that you're not vain about it, but you shouldn't deny it, either."

"I'm too skinny and I'm all scarred up."

"No one sees those scars under your clothes. And you're not as skinny as you used to be, either." Darcy smiled. "In fact, I think you're beginning to develop a figure."

"Not like other girls."

"You may be behind some of the other girls physically, but you're catching up fast," Darcy said. "It might not seem like it sometimes, but you're growing up."

Taylor blushed. "Can I ask you a question?"

"Of course."

"My mom and I have talked about this stuff, but I still have questions…and she's not here."

"You can ask me anything." Darcy felt such tenderness toward the girl it was all she could do not to pull her into her lap and cradle her, the way she had Riley when he was afraid or hurt or confused. But after all their talk of growing up, Taylor might think she was too old.

"What's it like to get a period?" Taylor asked. "I mean, people say it doesn't hurt, but how could it not?"

"I'll try to explain, though your father is probably better at anatomy than I am."

"It's just too embarrassing to talk to my dad about this stuff," Taylor said. "Besides, he's a guy. How can he really know what he's talking about if he's never had one?"

"Good point." There followed a conversation Darcy had never thought she'd have, about cramps and PMS and sanitary napkins and all the things involved with a girl growing into a woman. When she'd answered all of Taylor's questions and the girl thanked her, Darcy did pull her close. "I'm glad I could be here for you," she said. Since she'd lost Riley, she thought she might never feel so needed by someone else again. So trusted and, yes, loved.

MIKE COULDN'T IMAGINE what Darcy and Taylor were up to, sequestered in Taylor's room for so long. Were they playing computer games or talking about dancing? Were they talking about *him?*

He tried to focus on the hockey game on television, showing them he didn't care what they were up to, but he might have been watching a curling competition for all he paid attention to the screen. Every sense was focused on the closed door of the bedroom down the hall.

When he'd answered the bell and found Darcy standing there, his first instinct had been to send her away. His and Taylor's lives had been comfortable and relatively trouble-free before Darcy stepped into the picture. Taylor didn't get into fights at school or obsess over belly dancing costumes, and Mike certainly didn't punch out strangers in restaurants or lie awake nights thinking about curvy blondes who could swivel their hips in ways designed to drive a man wild.

But tonight, as had happened so often before, what Mike's brain told him to do and how his body responded were in direct opposition. It wasn't only lust that made him hold his tongue and let Darcy in to see Taylor. She had an essential goodness that made him ashamed of blaming her for something he should have addressed with Taylor himself. After all, Taylor was his daughter and they'd always been close. He should have picked up on how much the appearance thing was bothering her and done more to reassure her.

The bedroom door opened and Darcy stepped into the hall. "Taylor wants you to come kiss her good-night," she said.

He entered the room and found a girl transformed. Taylor smiled at him for the first time in two days and held her arms out for a hug. "It's good to see you feeling better," he said as he embraced her.

"Darcy and I had a long talk," she said. "She explained all about boys being weird, and about how all the changes in my body are making me feel weird, too."

He started to remind her she could have talked to him, but stopped himself. Much as he tried, he could never have explained things the way Darcy had, from a woman's perspective. "Do you think I'm weird?" he asked.

She giggled. "Only sometimes."

Fair enough. He kissed her good-night, and returned to the living room, glad to see Darcy was still there. "Can I get you anything to drink?" he asked.

"A cup of tea might be nice," she said.

"I'll see if I have any." He rummaged in the cabinet and came up with a boxed assortment of herbal teas Taylor had gotten on a school field trip to the

Celestial Seasonings plant in Boulder. "Chamomile, peppermint or lemon?"

"Peppermint."

He decided to stick with water and brought both drinks back to the living room. "Thanks for stopping by tonight," he said.

"I was afraid you'd think I was interfering in something that was none of my business."

"You made Taylor feel better, and that's what counts." He rubbed the back of his neck. "It's hard for me to admit I can't be everything to her."

"You do your best. Tonight, she needed a woman's perspective." She set the teacup on the coffee table. "I care about Taylor. I care about you, too."

Once more he acted without thinking, sliding over closer and pulling her into his arms. She responded with all the warmth and passion he remembered from their previous kisses.

"I care about you, too," he said, his voice rough with emotion. "I'll admit it makes me nervous."

"Why is that?"

"For so long, I haven't had room in my life for anyone but Taylor," he said. "She was so sick and all my energy was directed toward getting her well."

"But she's better now."

"Yes. And medications can help prevent rejection. But they can't guarantee it, and the treatments themselves have side effects that might damage other organs." He shook his head. "She could live a healthy, normal life or she could get sick again tomorrow."

"Every one of us is fragile that way."

He sensed her own fragility. She'd endured so much, yet how much had that cost her? They kissed again, a long, tender exchange. She shifted to press more closely to him, and he put one hand on her hip, feeling the curve of her body through her jeans.

His heart pounded with desire and fear. There had been no other woman in his life since Melissa. Yes, their divorce had been for the best, but that didn't mean it hadn't wounded the part of him that had believed the vows he'd made that their love would last "till death do us part."

"After Riley and Pete died, I told myself I deserved to be alone," Darcy whispered, her lips against his throat, the words felt as much as heard. "I'd made bad choices and obviously didn't know how to have a healthy relationship."

He cradled the side of her face and lifted her head until her eyes met his. "Maybe it's time to try again," he said.

"Maybe it is."

They kissed hungrily, tongues entwined, bodies pressed together. He could feel himself slipping further from the reality of his living room into the promise of the fantasies that had haunted his dreams.

It took everything in him to pull away from her. "I'd ask you to stay, but…"

"I know. And I'd take you up on that offer, if we could." She stood, straightening her clothes, smoothing her hair, the innocent gestures making him only want her more. "I'd better go."

He walked her to the door, where they kissed again, pressed against the wall like lovers who wouldn't make it to the bedroom before they tore their clothes off.

She was the one who pushed him away this time. "See you soon," she said, and slipped out of the door before he could convince himself it would be all right for her to stay, even if Taylor was right down the hall.

He stood at the door a long time after she drove away.

IF THAT EVENING of kisses on Mike's couch had accomplished nothing else, it had resulted in Taylor's return to the Wednesday afternoon dance class. Her fight with Nathan had apparently made her something of a school celebrity, and she wore her bruise like a badge of honor. "Purple is my favorite color," she said when Debby pointed out that Taylor's eye matched her sweater.

"Are you going to have a purple costume for the show?" Hannah asked.

"Maybe," Taylor said. She looked anxiously at Darcy, who winked.

After class, she ushered Taylor to the sewing room.

Mike had agreed to let Taylor stay late again today to work on her costume. Afterward, Darcy would drive the girl home. "I've been working while you were away," Darcy said. "I still need to hem the skirt and add some sequins, but I want to know what you think."

She'd sewn a simple cropped top out of the purple glitter material and added long, full sleeves that ended in a ruffle at the wrist. To this she'd added a panel of flesh-colored knit that reached to the waist, also dusted with glitter. A row of silver sequins at the neck and bottom of the crop top gave it more sparkle.

"It's beautiful," Taylor said, eyes wide.

"Try it on." Darcy handed her the matching skirt, trimmed with more glitter and sequins.

Taylor darted into the bathroom. "Do you need any help?" Darcy called through the door.

"No, I'm okay."

She emerged a few moments later, walking on tiptoe, arms held out from her sides, as if at any moment she might execute a ballerina twirl. "How does it look?" she asked anxiously.

"Gorgeous." Darcy covered her mouth with one hand, sudden tears stinging her eyes and the back of her throat. Taylor was a princess straight out of a Disney movie.

"You think this bottom part is okay?" Taylor smoothed the spangled knit over her stomach.

"From the stage, no one will even know it's

fabric," Darcy said. "And even up close it looks very natural."

"Like those ice-skaters," Taylor said.

"Better. Like a belly dancer. What do you think?"

"I love it." She threw her arms around Darcy, surprising her with the strength of her hug. "Thank you so much! It's the best present ever."

Darcy put one hand on the girl's back, and stroked her hair with the other. She closed her eyes, savoring the weight and warmth of a small body clinging to her, of a child's love radiating through her. Remembering...

Taylor pushed away, breaking the spell, and began to twirl, the skirt flaring around her legs. "It's the most beautiful costume ever. I can't wait to show Dad and the other girls."

"I thought maybe we should surprise him at the show." Darcy wasn't sure if Mike was ready to see his daughter dressed as a belly dancer, even if the costume wasn't at all revealing.

"Yes!" Taylor clapped her hands together. "He's going to be so surprised when he sees me."

"You should have someone waiting with a camera. Now hop up here." Darcy patted the chair beside her. "I need to measure the hem."

Darcy measured and pinned, then Taylor changed back into her jeans and sweater. Darcy tucked the costume into the closet with all her outfits. "You can stay after class again next week," she said. "We'll check the hem and add any finishing touches you think the costume needs." It was time to drive to Mike's office. Darcy wished she could drive slower, to make her time alone with Taylor last longer.

"I knew Dad didn't mean it when he said I shouldn't dance anymore," Taylor said. "He always acts like that when I try new things he thinks might hurt me. He was the same way about skiing. The first time I wanted to go skiing after my surgery he was worried I'd get too tired or too cold or I'd fall, or all the people there would have too many germs. It took forever for me to talk him into letting me go."

"Are you a good skier?"

"Pretty good. I'd be better if I could go more often. I wish we could live in our condo in Breckenridge all winter, but it's too far from Dad's office."

The mining town turned ski resort was a picture postcard place of restored historic buildings and colorful new ones against the backdrop of snow-covered peaks.

"We're going this weekend," Taylor said. "I can hardly wait. I hope we get lots and lots of snow."

A weekend she wouldn't see them.

"Are you dancing this weekend?" Taylor asked.

"No, I have the weekend off." March was a notoriously slow time of year. She was doing transcription at home for a law firm to fill in the gap in her income.

"You should come skiing with us!" Taylor strained against her seat belt.

Darcy felt a flutter of excitement. "Your father might have other ideas," she said. She parked and shut off the engine, wondering what Mike would think of the prospect of the two of them—the three of them—spending the weekend together.

"We'll ask him now," Taylor said, unbuckling her seat belt.

"Taylor, I don't know…" But the girl was already out of the car, racing up the driveway. By the time Darcy reached the front door, Taylor was there with Mike. "Daddy, can Darcy come skiing with us this weekend, please?"

Darcy felt his eyes on her. She couldn't read his expression. Their eyes met only briefly before he returned his attention to Taylor.

"I asked and she's not dancing this weekend and she likes to ski and the condo has plenty of room," Taylor said in a rush.

"Your mother sent a package for you from Italy. I put it in your room." He patted her shoulder. "Why don't you go check it out while Darcy and I talk?"

He waited until Taylor had shut the door behind her before he turned and pulled Darcy into his arms.

By the time he raised his head they were both breathless. "I've been wanting to do that ever since you left my house last week," he said.

"Mmm." She stroked his cheek, the sharp bristles

of his five-o'clock shadow rasping against her palm. "You know where I live."

"It hardly seemed appropriate to make out with a ten-year-old in tow, and I couldn't think of a good excuse to abandon my patients during the day."

She nodded. "My students might have been shocked at your sudden appearance, as well."

He kissed her again, and she arched against him, loving the feel of his body, hard and muscular, against hers.

"So will you come with us to Breck this weekend?" he asked.

"I'd love to." A full weekend of sun, snow and Mike's kisses. It would be tough, behaving themselves in front of Taylor, but Darcy had always liked a challenge.

CHAPTER TEN

"LOOK HOW HARD it's snowing, Dad. Isn't it great?" Taylor said, her nose pressed to the car window. It looked as if someone was emptying out hundreds of feather pillows. The tops of cars, shrubs and fire hydrants were quickly disappearing beneath the onslaught.

Mike carefully maneuvered the car over the barely visible pavement. "I don't think the weathermen predicted such a big storm for this morning," he said.

"I hope it's snowing in Breckenridge," Taylor said. "It'll be great for skiing." She turned from the window. "I don't know how I'll sit through school. I wish I could skip just this one Friday and we could go to Darcy's house and leave now."

"Darcy and I have work to do, and your job is to go to school," Mike said. "Three-thirty will be here before you know it." He'd agreed to take off early to drive to the mountains.

"I'm so glad Darcy can come with us," Taylor said. "It'll be so much fun to be with her all weekend."

Mike had hardly slept last night, his thoughts too full of everything that might happen this weekend, and everything he wanted to happen. Darcy still had the power to throw him off balance, but he was growing accustomed to the feeling, and even looked forward to it. At almost forty it was exciting to think a woman could inspire new feelings in him.

He followed a bus into the school driveway. Traffic was lighter than usual. Even Taylor's usual carpool buddy, Curtis Askew, had decided to stay home. "I'll see you at three-thirty," Mike said, as Taylor unbuckled her seat belt and leaned forward for her goodbye kiss.

"With this snow, maybe they'll dismiss us early," she said.

"I still have to see all my patients before we can leave."

"Maybe the snow will make your patients cancel their appointments and stay home." She slid out of the car. "Bye, Dad. See you soon." Backpack over one shoulder, she disappeared into the mass of students and swirling snow.

The weather certainly wasn't keeping any patients home this morning. By the time Mike arrived at his office the waiting room was full and Nicole greeted him with a stack of charts. "Typical Friday 'I need to get well before the weekend' stuff," she said.

He nodded. People might let their kids limp along all week with symptoms, hoping they'd get better on their own, but the prospect of a weekend wiped out by illness drove them to the doctor, hoping for an instant cure he was rarely able to offer.

He worked steadily all morning, snow forgotten. At noon he retreated to his office to wolf down the sandwich Peggy ordered from the deli down the street and was surprised to see a near whiteout outside his window. Traffic to the resort would be a nightmare. Any sane person would stay home. But he had a little girl and a woman who were looking forward to this weekend. And he'd spent his life driving in the snow. If they took it slowly, they'd get there fine, but the sooner they left, the better.

An hour later, the school called. "They're releasing classes early," Peggy told him. "Taylor wants to know if she can ride the bus to Darcy's house."

"Yes, that's a good idea." He had Taylor's ski gear and suitcase in the car with his own things. He could swing by Darcy's without making the extra trip back to his house.

At two he took another break and checked the highway department Web site. Plows were keeping the major highways clear and though traffic into the high country was moving slowly, it was moving. "Heavy snow is expected into the night," the site informed him.

"How many more patients?" he asked Nicole. If he could wrap it up here, they could get started well before dark.

"Two. Nothing major." She smiled. "We'll have you off to your romantic weekend in no time."

"I'm taking my daughter skiing, Nicole."

"And that dancer is going along to babysit?" Nicole laughed. "Have a good time, Dr. Mike. You deserve it."

"Mrs. Jankowski is on line one," Peggy interrupted them, no humor at all in her expression. "She says Brent is ill."

Mike took the call. "I'm so sorry to bother you on a Friday afternoon," Sarah Jankowski began. "I wouldn't have called, but the school sent Brent home today with a horrible cough and he says he's not feeling well."

"How long has he had this cough?"

"Well, he coughs some all the time, you know. Since that last bout of bronchitis it's almost like a habit with him. But this is different—deeper. And he says it hurts."

"You'd better bring him in."

"It'll be a bit before I can get there, with this weather."

"That's all right. I'll wait." He hung up, sighing. So much for getting away early. But he couldn't let Brent go the weekend with a possible return of his bronchitis—or something worse.

He let Peggy and Nicole know Brent was on his way, then picked up the phone again and punched in Darcy's number. "Hello," she greeted him. "Taylor phoned and said she's taking the bus to my house, so we'll be ready when you get here."

"I have an emergency patient coming in, so I'm going to be late," he said. "I've been monitoring the traffic and weather reports and while things seem to be okay now, as it gets dark they're bound to get worse. I was wondering if you wanted to take Taylor and head on up to the condo. I'll follow in my car when I wrap things up here."

"Oh." Pause. "Are you sure you don't want us to wait for you?"

"I'd feel better knowing you and Taylor were safely out of here in daylight. I should only be a couple hours behind you. That is, if you're okay driving in the snow."

"Oh, yes. I did a birthday party during the Blizzard of 2003, and you'd be surprised how many people still show up at a restaurant when the weather's bad. It's like no one wants to get trapped at home, so they all head out."

"It's freeway almost all the way to Breck, so you should be fine." He gave her directions to the condo. "Taylor knows it well, so she'll help you find it and show you where to park," he said. "I'll be up there as soon as I can."

"I'll look forward to it."

Simple words, but there was an extra heat behind them that sent a shiver of anticipation through him.

Damn Brent's cough. He hated to be away from Darcy one moment more than necessary.

DARCY STOOD at her front window, watching a world covered in white. The snowflakes were smaller than they'd been this morning, more powdered sugar than feathers. She'd been truthful when she told Mike she had plenty of experience driving in snow, but she hadn't told him she dreaded going out in it.

It had been snowing the night Pete and Riley had died—a storm much like this one, not a full-out blizzard, just steady, heavy snowfall. She hadn't thought twice about driving to the party where she was the featured entertainment.

She would never know what possessed Pete to head toward his buddy's house in the mountains. If Darcy had been home, she would have kept Riley with her. If she'd known Pete was drinking, she would have taken his keys. If only…

A small figure materialized in the snow, struggling up the driveway. Darcy opened the door and ran out to greet Taylor, taking her backpack and ushering her into the kitchen, where she helped her out of her parka and snow boots. "There's so much snow!" the girl said, wide-eyed. "Skiing's going to be awesome."

"Your father called and he has to work late," Darcy said.

"No!" Taylor's face crumpled. "It's not fair."

"No, it's not. But he asked me to go ahead and

take you to the condo. He'll meet us there in a few hours."

"Yay!" Taylor jumped from the bench and hugged Darcy. "I wish Dad could come with us right away, but it'll be fun to go there, just the two of us."

"Sure it will." Not fun, exactly, but she was grateful she'd have the girl to distract her. "Let's go ahead and have a snack, then you can take your medicine and help me load the car."

Traffic was light through town, and the snow had all but stopped, so Darcy began to relax. In the backseat, Taylor chattered about the A she'd gotten on a history test, the spider that had emptied out the girls' locker room during sixth period, and skiing.

"I want to learn to slide rails in the terrain park, but Dad won't let me," she said. "He thinks it's too dangerous."

"It looks dangerous to me." Darcy moved into the right lane to allow a snowplow to pass.

"But lots of kids do it. And I have a helmet."

You're not lots of kids, Darcy wanted to say. But she didn't. It was the sort of thing adults said that children hated to hear. Besides, every time Taylor looked at her scars or took her handfuls of pills she was reminded of how different she was from other children. Of how unfair life could be.

The freeway was plowed and the snow had stopped. They should have had a smooth drive all the way to Breckenridge, but Darcy had driven only a few miles when traffic came to a standstill. Three lanes of glowing red taillights curved ahead as far as the eye could see, eighteen-wheeler trucks idling alongside SUVs with ski racks and economy cars topped with snowboards.

"What's going on?" Taylor asked.

"I don't know. An accident, maybe?" Darcy reached for her phone and punched in the number for the highway department. A recorded voice informed her that due to weather conditions there were a number of road closures in the area, including the freeway they were traveling.

Darcy hung up the phone and sighed. "The road's closed."

"Closed? But it's stopped snowing."

"There's been an avalanche. They're detouring people onto a side road and back the way we came." She inched the car forward as everyone ahead of her did the same.

"That's okay," Taylor said. "We can go the back way. I'll show you."

The back way was an alternative route into the mountains, down a winding, two-lane state highway. The road passed sleepy ranches and a few small towns. In the summer it was a pleasant, scenic drive. In the winter it was lonely and could be treacherous.

"I don't know," Darcy said. "Maybe we should contact your father and see what he wants to do." Mike may have finished with his patients, then he could take over the driving. Darcy would feel safe with him at the wheel.

"He said to go ahead and he'd meet us later," Taylor said. "I can show you the road to take. It's easy."

"I know the way," Darcy said. It was the route Pete had taken the night of the accident. A route that would take her right by the place where his car had plunged off the road. Darcy had avoided driving the road ever since that night.

As they continued to creep forward with the traffic, she picked up the phone again and called Mike. "Hi. This is Dr. Mike Carter. Leave a message and I'll get back to you."

She hung up without speaking, and turned up the heater against the chill that numbed her from the inside out.

"Dad keeps his phone off when he's with patients," Taylor said. "Somebody else probably came in and needed him. He can't turn sick people away. Doctors take an oath about that."

Darcy imagined Mike explaining this to Taylor, how he had to help people because of the promise he'd made when he'd received his medical license.

"We'll go the back way," she said. She wouldn't think of the bad things that had happened on that road. She'd focus instead on all the good things that lay ahead.

"THE CONGESTION IS definitely back, Mrs. Jankowski, but I'm not sure it's bronchitis this time." Mike moved his stethoscope slowly across Brent's back, listening to his constricted breathing.

"What do you think it is?" Sarah Jankowski held the boy's shirt, wringing it like a dish towel.

"It could be pneumonia." It could also be congestive heart failure, but he didn't like to raise that alarm without more proof. "I want to send you to the hospital for a chest X-ray and some blood work."

"The hospital? Can it wait until Monday?"

If only everything could wait until Monday, until after his weekend with Darcy and Taylor. "I'm afraid not. I'll have Nicole call ahead and let them know you're coming."

After he'd explained to Nicole what he wanted and Brent and his mother were on their way, Mike retreated to his office and tried to call Darcy. Out the window he could see the snow had stopped, so traffic should be clearing.

Her phone went straight to voice mail. Good for her, not driving and trying to talk on the phone. But the depth of his disappointment at not being able to speak to her surprised him.

There was a knock on his office door. "Come in."

Peggy stuck her head in. "I just heard an avalanche above Georgetown has closed Interstate 70."

"An avalanche?" He stood. "Darcy and Taylor were headed that way."

"The only injury was to a truck driver and he's

going to be okay. They've diverted everyone else. The only way to Breckenridge now is along Highway 285 to Highway 9."

He sat again. "Taylor and I have driven that route sometimes. There's that one bad patch through South Park, but after that it's fine."

"I don't care much for Hoosier Pass."

"I'm sure Darcy's a careful driver," he said.

"Oh, I'm sure. What do you think is wrong with Brent?"

"I'm worried his heart is failing," Mike admitted. "He's caught an infection he can't shake and the damaged heart muscle can't compensate. I've got a call into Dr. Munroe for his opinion." Munroe was the pediatric cardiologist who'd cared for Taylor.

"I hope he's okay," Peggy said.

"Me, too." He hoped everyone was okay, but knew too well that life seldom granted that kind of peace, where everyone you cared about was safe and happy and well, all at the same time.

He checked the clock on his desk. Five o'clock. Not so late. Brent would have his tests, Mike would talk to Dr. Munroe and, if necessary, turn Brent's care over to the specialist. In a few hours he'd be in Breckenridge, enjoying a nice steak and a glass of wine across the table from Darcy, looking forward to what might happen later, when Taylor was tucked into bed....

IT STARTED to snow again just past the town of Bailey. The snowflakes seemed to fly right at the windshield, a swirl of white confetti against the growing darkness, glittering in the headlights. "It's like we're in the middle of a giant snow globe," Taylor said.

"Then I wish whoever owns the thing would stop shaking it," Darcy said.

"But it's so pretty."

Any other time, Darcy might have agreed. The world was covered in white frosting, all the sharp edges softened, even the sound of the car's tires muted by snow.

The car slowed as the transmission shifted to a lower gear. They climbed a steep hill. The road curved toward the top, threading between a rocky cliff and a steep drop-off.

Pete's car had landed at the bottom of that drop-off, rolling an estimated six times before it landed, upright, in a pasture where bison grazed.

Sometimes, horrible as it sounded, she was glad Pete had died. Even that grief was easier to bear than the thought of him having lived while Riley hadn't. She didn't think she would have been able to forgive him.

She still hadn't forgiven him, just as she couldn't forgive herself.

She was crying by the time she reached the top of the hill, tears streaming down her face. She tilted her head forward, her hair falling across one cheek, hiding her face from the child in the backseat. She prayed Taylor didn't notice her distress in the gathering darkness.

Taylor. She fixed her thoughts on the girl. The child with Riley's heart. Taylor had a gentleness and a vulnerability Darcy's rough, tough boy had never possessed. She was a child, yet all she'd suffered gave her a maturity that showed up at unexpected moments. Sometimes when Darcy looked at Taylor, she saw her own insecurities and doubts staring back at her.

She slowed the car to a crawl at the top of the hill, forcing her foot to stay in contact with the accelerator, gripping the steering wheel so tightly her knuckles were white, grateful for the darkness and the swirling snow that prevented her from seeing beyond the reach of the headlights.

And then they were past the danger point. The curve straightened and the highway descended gradually toward the lights of Fairplay, laid out along the river like a Victorian mining town.

Shaky with relief, Darcy guided the car into the lot of the first business she saw, a combination gas station/liquor store/coffee shop.

"Why are we stopping?" Taylor asked.

"I need a break." Darcy pried her stiff fingers from the steering wheel and fumbled with her seat belt. "Hot chocolate sounds good, don't you think?"

"Hot chocolate sounds great."

Taylor met Darcy outside the car as she unfolded from the front seat. Darcy still felt wobbly, so she put one hand on the door to steady herself, and the other on the girl. She drew Taylor close and gave her a quick hug.

"What was that for?" the girl asked.

"I'm just glad you're here with me," she said. Glad life had given her a second chance to get things right.

CHAPTER ELEVEN

MIKE HUNCHED over the steering wheel, trying to make out the road through the swirling snow. Traffic crawled up the steep grade of the last of three passes he had to cross to get to Breckenridge. Visibility was so poor all he could do was follow the taillights of the car in front of him and hope they didn't lead him over a cliff.

This was insane. Any man with sense would get a hotel room and wait for the storm to pass. Or better yet, he would never have left home in the first place. But there was nothing for Mike at his empty house; Taylor and Darcy waited in Breckenridge.

Chest X-rays had shown mild congestion in Brent's lungs, and the blood work had revealed a slightly elevated white count, a sign of infection, though not a severe one. Mike had prescribed antibiotics and a decongestant and sent the boy and his mother home with instructions to report to the emergency room if Brent's symptoms worsened.

Darcy had called Mike just before he left Wood-bine, to let him know they'd arrived safely. She'd sounded so calm, as if driving ninety miles in a blizzard was something she did every day. Listening to her made him feel better about the long drive ahead.

He remembered one of the last trips he'd made to the condo while he and Melissa were still married. Melissa was never a shrew, but she didn't like being inconvenienced. She'd complained about the heavy traffic, pointing out if they'd left earlier they could have avoided the backup. She'd chided Mike for driving too close, then made disapproving noises when he let another car cut in front of him. She'd frowned over the crowded condition of the parking garage, which had forced them to park far from the elevator. Mike began to think of her as a black cloud, casting gloom all around her.

In contrast, Darcy was full of sunlight.

He held on to that thought as he guided the car down the opposite side of Hoosier Pass and on into the town of Breckenridge. The lights of the condos and shops sparkled in the snow like Christmas decorations. A few people moved along the snowy sidewalks between the restaurants and bars, and a white shuttle bus chugged slowly away from a stop.

He found a parking space in the condo garage and carried his duffel bag and ski boots to the elevator. He felt as weary as if he'd walked all the way from Woodbine. A quick check of his watch showed it was nine o'clock. Taylor should be in bed, though part of him hoped she'd waited up for him.

He was fumbling with his key in the door when it opened. "Daddy, you're finally here!"

Taylor, in flannel pajamas and fuzzy pink slippers, stood on tiptoe to embrace him. He dropped the bag and his boots and scooped her up, breathing in the smell of strawberry shampoo.

As he straightened he saw Darcy. She wore yoga pants and a light knit top—a sexier version of sweats—her long hair loose about her shoulders. "I hope your drive wasn't too bad," she said.

"It was horrible, but that doesn't matter now that I'm here." He shifted Taylor to his right hip and held out his left arm. Darcy came to him and he hugged her, eyes closed, savoring the moment.

Taylor squirmed, reminding him his daughter—and his back—couldn't hold the pose that long. "I'm glad you waited up for me," he told Taylor as he set her on the floor once more. "But isn't it past your bedtime?"

"I want to stay up with you and Darcy," she said.

"You'll see plenty of me and Darcy tomorrow. And if you don't get enough sleep you'll be a big grouch. Come on, I'll tuck you in."

"While you do that, I'll reheat your dinner," Darcy said.

He shed his coat, then carried his duffel to his room and Taylor to hers. She made no more protests, clearly weary from the excitement of the day. By the time he'd verified she'd taken her medications and brushed her teeth, pulled the covers up to her chin and kissed her good-night, her eyes were already drooping. He switched off the light and moved quietly down the hall and into the kitchen.

"Something smells good," he said, moving in close behind Darcy. He wanted to put his arms around her and pull her near, but wasn't sure how she'd react.

"Pork chops, hash browns and peas—all stuff I found in your freezer." She gave him an appreciative glance. "You keep things well stocked for a bachelor who doesn't visit here often."

"I like to eat, and I always have intentions of making it up here more, so at the beginning of the season I stocked up."

The microwave dinged and she reached up and took out a plate. "I hope you don't mind that it's reheated. Taylor and I ate earlier."

"I'm so hungry I could eat fried boot." He watched as she arranged the potatoes alongside the chops. If he'd been making the meal he'd have eaten everything from the pan.

"How is your patient?" she asked, carrying the plate to the table at the end of the counter. "The one you stayed to see?"

"Not too good." He sliced into a pork chop, suddenly starving. "It's a boy, a couple of years younger than Taylor, with a similar heart valve problem. I'm worried he's going into congestive heart failure, though the cardiologist didn't seem too concerned."

He frowned. The cardiologist had agreed with Mike's decision to prescribe medication and send Brent and his mother home. Mike would have rested easier if Brent had remained in the hospital for observation. He couldn't decide if his medical instincts were trying to alert him to a real problem, or if guilt over Taylor had him imagining disaster where there was none.

"I hope he's okay," Darcy said. "Would you like some wine? There's a bottle of red in your cabinet."

"I'd love some." After the third mountain pass he'd contemplated a stiff shot of Scotch, but the wine would do.

He continued eating while she opened the wine and filled two glasses. "To a lovely weekend," she said, and touched her glass to his.

"To a lovely weekend." He sipped the wine, which was smooth going down, warming him. "Another half a bottle of this and I might forget about that horrible drive."

"That bad?" she asked.

"The roads were almost invisible by the time I got to Hoosier Pass," he said. "How was it for you?"

She shook her head. "I still had daylight. In some ways, I think not being able to see would have made it easier for me." She stared at the wine, but didn't make a move to drink it. Something in her stillness disturbed him.

He laid aside his fork. "Why is that?"

"Pete and Riley were killed at Red Hill Pass," she

said. "They were on their way to see a friend of Pete's. I...I haven't driven past there since."

"Until today." His own afternoon's ordeal seemed petty next to all she'd faced. "I never would have insisted you drive Taylor by yourself if I'd known. Why didn't you say something?"

"I didn't want you to think I was a coward."

"I would never think that." She had faced tragedy with more courage than he imagined he'd be able to muster in similar circumstances.

"Thank you for saying that." She raised the glass to her lips and took a long drink, her eyes meeting his over the rim.

He saw all the pain in her eyes, and the courage that had somehow carried her through. "I'm sorry you had to go through that," he said. "I wish I could've been there with you."

"Some other time we'll make the drive together. I made it because Taylor was with me—and because I wanted to be with you this weekend more than I wanted to be home alone. I'm tired of grief being the strongest emotion in my life."

He pushed aside his plate and reached across the table to take her hand. "You're the bravest woman I've ever met," he said. "Every day you face things I can only imagine."

"I'm tired of being brave." The heat in her voice caught him off guard.

"Then don't be," he said quietly. He stood and pulled her up with him, into his arms.

She melted against him, her kisses searing him, banishing the last ice around his heart.

He pressed her back against the counter. She wasn't wearing a bra and when he slid his hand beneath her sweater and felt her bare breast he groaned.

"Shh," she whispered. "Taylor will hear."

"No she won't. She's exhausted from the excitement. She'll sleep all night." He wouldn't use his daughter as an excuse to keep them apart any longer.

He kissed her neck, sucking on the sweet, smooth flesh. "My bedroom is at the other end of the condo. Darcy, I want to make love to you. I think I've wanted it practically from the moment we met, but now that I know you better I only want you more."

"Yes. I want that, too."

"The world won't end if Taylor finds out we spent the night together. She loves you. I love you."

"Oh, Mike." She smiled, eyes glittering. Then she let him take her hand and lead her to the bedroom.

DARCY FELT the same butterflies she got before she debuted a new dance. She reminded herself sex was not a solo performance. Rather, it was a duet. She only hoped she could remember her part.

"You're trembling," Mike said as he took her in his arms after he'd locked the bedroom door behind them.

"I'm nervous," she admitted. "It's been a while."

"For me, too." He held her, her head cradled on his shoulder. "I don't think it's something we forget. But if we do, we can help each other remember."

He kissed her again, almost tentatively, hands that had explored her so boldly before hesitating at the hem of her sweater, as if the short walk from the kitchen had given him too much time to think about what they were doing.

She'd had a dance teacher early on who'd told her the reason she wasn't getting any better as a performer was that she thought too much about the moves she needed to do and not enough about how the music made her feel. If she focused more on her emotions, her training would take over and the moves would come naturally.

That teacher had been right. Darcy gripped the hem of her sweater, lifted it over her head and sent it sailing across the room. Not looking at Mike, she also stripped off the pants, and stood before him naked.

When she did meet his eyes he was smiling, and she felt warmed in the heat of his gaze. "So much for taking it slow," he said.

"We've wasted so much time already." She undid the top button of his shirt.

He kissed her again while she fumbled with the buttons, tracing the curves of her hips and thighs as she pulled the shirttails from his pants and pushed it back off his shoulders.

Then it was her turn. She kissed her way down his chest as he struggled out of the shirt, removed his belt and lowered the zipper over the hard length of his erection.

The butterflies returned at this blatant evidence of his desire, but they were soon vanquished by her own longing. It had been so long since she'd loved and been loved. Too long.

She kissed him with new intensity, clinging to him, reveling in the feel of flesh against flesh. Her urgency fueled his desire and soon they were rolling on the bed like randy teens, but with an adult's knowledge of what lay ahead.

"You are so beautiful," he said when they paused to catch their breath. He smoothed his hand across her belly. "So gorgeous."

Never mind that her stomach wasn't as flat as she would like or her breasts as round. With him she felt gorgeous, and that was all that mattered. That, and the delicious tension building inside her.

Still, she held him off. "I trust a doctor has condoms?"

"This weekend, I do." He got up and went into the bathroom, leaving her with the knowledge that he'd had plans to make love to her this weekend. Taylor might have extended the invitation, but Mike definitely wanted her along.

He'd said he loved her. Magic words that had left her completely undone. "I love you, too," she whispered, the words hard to say, even when he wasn't around to hear them.

Then he was back, stalking across the room naked, stripping open a condom package as he approached. He knelt over her, fitting it on, then she reached for him.

"Are you sure you're ready?" he asked, caressing her thighs.

"I'm more than ready," she said. "All I want is you in me."

"I'm always happy to give a lady what she wants." The roguish gleam in his eye made her laugh, then he made her gasp as he filled her. Such exquisite pleasure...

She quit thinking about moves and focused on feeling, letting her body lead the way. What pleased her brought pleasure to him, strengthening the connection between them.

The intensity of her climax caught her by surprise, and she bit the side of her hand to keep from crying out. Then Mike covered her lips with his own, smothering his own groans.

When he finally released her, sliding over to lie by her side, she couldn't stop smiling, despite her tears.

"Are you crying?" Mike asked.

"Only because I'm so happy." She rolled onto her side to face him. "Mike, you don't know. There was a time I imagined I could never be this happy again."

"Me, too." He drew her close, to cradle her head in the hollow of his shoulder. "Me, too."

Then he fell asleep.

She rested her palm on his chest, feeling the steady, strong beat of his heart. "I love you," she whispered, even though she knew he couldn't hear her.

VERY EARLY in the morning, Darcy woke up and slipped from Mike's bed. She found her sweater and yoga pants on the floor, put them on and tiptoed from the room.

She had thought to retire to the spare bedroom, but she was too restless to go back to bed—or at least to a cold bed, alone. Instead, she went to Taylor's room.

The girl slept on her back, one arm flung out at her side, curls falling across her face. How often had Darcy stood over her son and watched him sleep like this? She'd missed the privilege of observing a child so innocent and still.

She resisted the urge to brush the hair from the girl's eyes, and contented herself with watching the even rise and fall of Taylor's chest.

That Taylor was alive to take a breath was a miracle. To think that one person's heart could be given to another, that this essential organ could live on after the one who had been born with it was gone....

But was that any more miraculous than Darcy's own restoration? She had gone through the motions of living after Riley and Pete died, but inside she had felt empty and hollow.

Yet here she was, so full of love she wanted to shout.

"Is everything all right?" Mike's voice behind her was soft. He moved to the bed. "Did Taylor call out?"

"No, she's fine," Darcy whispered. She tucked her arm in his. He was wearing only sweatpants, a marked change from the dress shirts and slacks she was used to seeing him in. He looked very sexy, and she felt the pleasant warmth of desire.

"I just like watching her," she whispered. "She's so beautiful."

"She is." Mike looked at his daughter a moment longer, then turned to Darcy. "So are you."

He laced his fingers with hers and led her from the room, back down the hall to his own bed. "I thought I should go into the guest room," Darcy said.

"We can go there. But the bed here is much more comfortable."

"Are you sure you don't want to go back to sleep?" she teased.

"I can't get enough of you." He pulled her close, letting her feel how ready he was for her again.

"Mmm." She swiveled her hips against him.

"What do you call that move?"

"An omi." She did it again—contracting the muscles first on her right side, then the center, then the left, releasing in the back, an undulating circle of movement around her hips.

"Very interesting." He grasped her hips.

"I know lots of interesting moves."

"I think you need to show me."

He let her take the lead in their lovemaking this time. She felt free to be in turns silly and serious, playful and passionate. She bit his shoulder when she came this time, and he stifled his cries against her breast.

"One day, Taylor will have an overnight stay with her mother," he said as they lay in each other's arms afterward. "Then I'll really show you. No holding back."

"If this is what you call holding back, I can't wait."

He kissed her again, the leisurely kiss of a man who is sure of what is his. But he abruptly stilled and pulled away. "Taylor's up."

"How do you know?"

"I heard the toilet flush."

Darcy tried to move quickly and quietly. She didn't feel what she and Mike had done was wrong, exactly, but she didn't want to start the day explaining things to a ten-year-old girl.

She hurried to the guest room to change while he headed for the kitchen. She found him there with Taylor twenty minutes later.

"Good morning, Darcy." Taylor greeted her with

a hug. "Dad's making pancakes." She giggled. "It's his specialty."

Darcy thought of a few other things the good doctor did especially well, but kept these thoughts to herself. "What are you grinning about?" Mike gave her a chaste kiss on the cheek and a not-so-chaste squeeze of her hip. "You don't think I can make pancakes?"

"I'm sure you can do anything you set your mind to."

"He can't make very good cookies," Taylor said. "He always burns the bottoms."

"It's just as well he isn't perfect," Darcy said. "Then he might be really hard to live with."

Mike's pancakes were indeed delicious. Darcy and Taylor polished off a stack each, then helped Mike with the dishes. "Let's go skiing!" Taylor shouted when they were done.

When Darcy thought about that morning later she wondered how much the fog of newfound love colored her memories. Everything about the morning was perfect in the way only dreams are perfect. The fresh snow was soft and smooth underfoot. The ski runs were long swatches of white corduroy. "You're a beautiful skier," Mike said when Darcy joined him at the bottom of a run.

"Thanks." His smile made her oblivious to the cold. Or maybe she was still warmed by this morning's lovemaking. Already she was looking forward to to-night…. But no, she shouldn't think that far ahead. She should simply enjoy this beautiful day. She turned to watch Taylor come down the hill. "You look great," she called to the girl.

"We should come skiing every weekend," Taylor said as the three of them glided into the lift line. "Or every day. You should quit your job at the clinic and we can move into the condo."

"And pay the rent with what?" Mike asked. "I'm too old to get by on good looks and charm."

"They probably need doctors in Breckenridge," Taylor said. "And belly dancers."

"Oh yes, there's a critical shortage of belly dancers," Darcy agreed. "It's why we're all so wealthy."

"Now you're just being silly," Taylor said.

"Yes, I am." They'd reached the front of the line and skied forward and waited for the chair.

When they were settled, the lap bar lowered, Taylor continued. "I still wish we could come up here more often."

"How long have you had the condo?" Darcy asked Mike, who sat on the other side of Taylor.

He stretched his arm along the back of the chair, his hand brushing Darcy's shoulder. "We bought it four years ago. At the time, I thought we'd be up here every weekend, but somehow we never make it more than a few times a season."

"Time gets away from us, doesn't it?" Had it really been a month since Mike and Taylor had changed her life? Being with them felt so right, as if she'd known them for years.

"Put the bar up, Dad," Taylor ordered as their chair approached the top of the lift. She scooted to the edge of the seat.

"Careful." Her father tugged at the back of her jacket. "We're not at the top yet."

"We are now!" As soon as they reached the unloading zone, Taylor hopped from the chair and sped away. Darcy dug in her poles, trying to build speed and keep up with the girl.

"Over here!" Taylor called, and waved from the top of a run.

Mike and Darcy skied over to Taylor, but as soon as they reached her side, she took off down the run. "Watch this!" She slid over to a mogul field at the side of the run. She wove in and out of the bumps with all the grace and speed of a raindrop flowing down a windowpane.

"Taylor, be careful!" Mike stopped beside Darcy. "She's not listening to me."

"She probably can't hear you."

"She doesn't want to hear me." He glanced at her. "I understand selective hearing is a common trait of adolescence. Not that a ten-year-old is an adolescent yet."

"She's a good kid." She started to tell him he had nothing to worry about, but that was a lie. There was always a new worry when it came to children.

They started down the slope, keeping to the groomed side of the run. Taylor was waiting for them halfway down. "Look at me," she said, and took off again. She hit the center of a bump and flew into the air, knees tucked and arms wide. Darcy held her breath and waited for Taylor to stick the landing, dimly aware of Mike next to her, swearing under his breath.

Taylor landed hard, but on her feet. She wobbled, then righted herself and turned to grin at them. Darcy laughed, and started toward her.

At that moment, Taylor lost her balance. She tipped over onto one ski, then fell and rolled, arms and legs flailing, like a character in a cartoon who turns into a giant snowball.

Darcy took off toward the girl, but Mike was in front of her, and reached Taylor's limp body first. She lay spread-eagle on her back, her ski poles still around her wrists, though she'd lost one ski. Her eyes were closed, her face flushed against the whiteness of the snow.

"Oh, God, is she all right?" Darcy covered her mouth with one mittened hand, as if she could hold back the awful words.

"Taylor, can you hear me?" Make clicked out of his skis and knelt beside his daughter. "Taylor!"

He touched her shoulder and she opened her eyes and grinned. "That was so awesome." She popped up like a jack-in-the-box. "It was almost like flying. Do you see my other ski?"

Darcy sagged against her ski poles. "You're all right."

"Of course I'm all right." Taylor awkwardly side-stepped up the slope to where her other ski jutted from the snow.

"Young lady, if you pull a stunt like that again, you will be grounded for a month," Mike said. His face was pale, the shadow of his dark beard stubble standing out against his skin.

"Aw, Dad, I didn't mean to scare you," Taylor said.

"What you did was dangerous and foolish and—"

"Why don't we go down and get some hot chocolate," Darcy interrupted.

"Yes!" Taylor clapped her hands together. She turned to her father.

Mike nodded. "Chocolate sounds good." As Taylor skied in front of them, he maneuvered over beside Darcy. "With maybe a double shot of schnapps in mine. I understand now why so many parents drink."

Darcy laughed. "She likes testing you, I think. But maybe she's not as fragile as she looks."

He shook his head. "All kids are more vulnerable than they feel, but try convincing them of that."

"I guess so. I remember when I first got my driver's license. I felt as if I could do anything."

"Then you wrecked the car," Mike said.

"No. But I ran out of gas and had to hike to a pay phone to call my dad to come get me. I was mortified."

"I wrecked the car," Mike said. "I had to work all summer to pay for the repairs."

At the lodge, Taylor raced around with two other girls and a boy, climbing the piles of snow and sliding down. Darcy waited at a picnic table in the sun while Mike went inside to fetch hot chocolate. "You have a beautiful daughter," an older woman said.

"Thank you." Darcy didn't correct her.

By noon they were all pink cheeked and it was clear Taylor was beginning to tire. "Let's go back to the condo and have lunch and a nap," Mike said. "This evening, we'll go tubing."

"Yay!" Taylor raised her hands in a victory gesture.

Darcy was heating soup while Mike grilled sandwiches when his cell phone rang. He went into the other room to take the call and returned a few minutes later, frowning. "That was my answering service," he said. "Brent Jankowski took a turn for the worse last night. His mother brought him to the emergency room this morning and he's been admitted."

"Is Brent the boy with the sick heart?" Taylor asked.

"Yes." Mike patted her shoulder. "I need to go see him. Tonight."

Darcy did her best to mask her disappointment. She wanted Mike to stay here with her, but of course he had to go and help this sick boy. "Taylor and I will do girl stuff," she said. "We can still go tubing when you get back."

"Thanks for understanding." He kissed her briefly on the lips, then kissed his daughter.

"I hope Brent is feeling better," Taylor said anxiously. "Is he as sick as I was?"

"Not quite," Mike said. "At least I hope not."

With Mike gone, the mood in the condo was definitely more subdued. Darcy and Taylor had lunch and Darcy left the dishes for later. "I could use a nap," she said, stifling a yawn. Her early morning and all that skiing were catching up with her.

"If you're tired, I guess I could lie down, too," Taylor said.

Darcy started for the guest room, but ended up instead in Mike's room. She crawled under the covers, imagining she could still smell the scent of his body and the faint musk of sex. She fell asleep smiling, wishing his arms were around her, but knowing he would be back.

CHAPTER TWELVE

"DARCY? I don't feel very good."

Darcy struggled up from a deep sleep. She'd been dreaming of Mike—of his arms wrapped around her, kissing his way down her body....

"Darcy!"

She opened one eye. Taylor stood by the side of the bed. "What is it, honey?" Darcy came more fully awake, both eyes open now. She pushed herself up on her elbows.

"I don't feel good," Taylor said, her face contorting.

Then she threw up on the bed.

Old skills long forgotten came rushing back. Darcy dodged the shower of vomit and within seconds she had a wet washrag and was cleaning a sobbing Taylor and escorting her back to bed. The child was burning up, but Darcy did her best not to show her concern. "Where does it hurt?" she asked, looking into Taylor's eyes as she tucked her in.

"My stomach and my head and my chest, a little."

"Your heart?" Darcy's voice rose.

"Behind it. When I try to take a deep breath there's a sharp tug."

Sharp tugs in the chest were not in Darcy's Mom repertoire. "Where does your dad keep the thermometer?" she asked.

"I don't know. I don't think we have one."

"I'll see if I can find it. You rest for a bit."

Back in the master bedroom, Darcy set about cleaning up the mess, holding her breath and somehow keeping from gagging. When the bed was stripped and the carpet scrubbed, she went in search of a thermometer.

The master bathroom was depressingly bare, with only a single unwrapped bar of soap and a package of toilet paper in the cabinet. Mike must carry his personal toiletries back and forth.

Taylor's bathroom was more cluttered, with a bottle of strawberry shampoo and another of grape bubble bath, along with a pharmacy's worth of medications.

Darcy's hand froze in the act of pushing aside a tall bottle of antacid. Taylor had thrown up her lunchtime meds. Had they been in her system long enough to do any good? Did she need to take them over again? Where was Mike when she needed him?

She groped in the back of the shelf and brushed against what she thought at first was a mini hair dryer or travel iron. On closer inspection, it proved to be one of those fancy ear thermometers like those used in doctors' offices.

Taylor lay on her side, sobbing quietly. "What is it, honey?" Darcy sat on the side of the bed and rubbed the girl's back.

"I want Daddy!" Taylor moaned.

"He'll be back soon. Just as soon as he can. Meanwhile, I'll look after you. I need to take your temperature, okay?"

Taylor nodded and Darcy inserted the thermometer in her ear. A hundred and three. Very high. She tried to remember what Riley's pediatrician had told her about fevers and children, but it was all a blur. She patted Taylor's back. "I'll see if I can find something in the kitchen to settle your stomach."

A search of the refrigerator and cabinets yielded nothing helpful. Mike had stocked the pantry, but not with a sick child in mind. Darcy called his cell phone. "Hi, this is Dr. Mike Carter. Leave a message and I'll get back to you."

She supposed the doctor was for the benefit of his answering service. She left a brief message and hung up. Maybe he was already on his way back, traveling through one of the areas where it was impossible to get a cell phone signal, or over an icy pass where it wasn't safe to answer the phone.

"Darcy!" Taylor's cry was weak but urgent.

Darcy raced back to the bedroom in time to see the child throw up again. "It's all right, honey. I'm here." She hurried to get another washrag, praying Mike would be back soon.

AT THE HOSPITAL MIKE STUDIED the latest results from the lab test he'd ordered for Brent. The numbers weren't nearly what he'd hoped for. "Fax these to Dr. Munroe," he said, returning the papers to the nurse at his elbow. The pediatric cardiologist had consulted by phone with Mike from his house in Aspen. Unlike Mike, he'd seen no need to make the drive back to Denver in yet another snowstorm.

"Keep the boy in the hospital for observation if it makes you feel better," he'd told Mike. "But he'll be fine until Monday."

Fine was a relative term when dealing with chronically ill children. *Fine* might be a lower temperature than usual or less pain than the child normally experienced.

His cell phone beeped, reminding him he had a message. He hit the voice mail button. "Mike, this is Darcy. I don't want to worry you, but Taylor has come down with some kind of bug. She's vomiting and has a fever of a hundred and three. I'm worried she might have thrown up her noon meds and I'm not sure what to do. I hope you'll be back soon."

He was already pulling on his coat by the time the message ended, punching in Darcy's number with his thumb while he searched for his gloves.

"Mike?" She answered on the second ring.

"I just got your message. What's up?"

"Mike, I'm so glad to hear from you. Are you on your way here?"

"I'm just leaving. What's going on with Taylor?"

He listened to her list of symptoms. "It sounds like the stomach flu that's been going around," he said. "Nasty stuff, but it usually resolves within a couple of days."

"Then you don't think it's serious?" He could hear her relief through the phone.

"You say she's not keeping down her medication?"

"She's not keeping down anything. The lunchtime doses were only in her for an hour before she threw up. Should I try to give her everything again?"

"No. Overdosing is as bad as underdosing in these cases. Just try to keep her quiet and I'll be there as fast as I can."

He hung up and finally found his gloves in his coat pocket. He put these on as he headed for the elevator.

"Dr. Carter, where are you going?" A young nurse—Daphne, he thought her name was—intercepted him near the elevators.

"I'm headed back to Breckenridge. My patient seems stable for now, but call me if you need anything."

"But you can't drive to Breckenridge," Daphne said. "It's a howling blizzard out there."

The storm Friday hadn't kept him from his daughter; he certainly wouldn't let a little more snow keep them apart. "I'm a good snow driver," he said. "Don't worry about me."

"I mean, you really can't go. All the roads are closed."

"They shut down I-70 again?" His shoulder muscles tensed as he thought of the torturous drive over three mountain passes on Highway 285.

"Yes. And they've closed 285 too. The news reports I heard said there were wrecks everywhere."

"The roads are closed," he repeated, numb.

"Yes. The police are advising people against even traveling locally. We're setting up all our empty rooms for personnel to spend the night here. I can see if there's something available for you."

"Do you know what the weather's like in Breckenridge?" he asked.

"Oh, I think the high country's getting lots of snow, too. The skiers are loving it."

The skiers might love it, but what if Taylor took a turn for the worse and needed advanced medical care? Breckenridge had a small hospital, but what if an ambulance couldn't get to her? Darcy had sounded pretty stressed on the phone just now. She didn't have any experience looking after a child as sick as Taylor could get.

He was Taylor's father. It was his responsibility

to look after her. He'd have to find a way, if he had to commandeer a team of sled dogs to take him to her.

"TAYLOR, HONEY, sit up and try to eat some toast and drink some of this tea," Darcy said.

"I don't want to."

"Honey, you have to. It's almost time to take your medicine again."

"I don't want to. I'll just throw up again." The girl pulled the covers over her head, like a small, burrowing animal retreating from a fox.

Darcy set the tray of tea and toast on the bedside table, fighting despair. If she were at home she'd try to tempt Taylor with Popsicles and cherry Jell-O, or ginger ale and saltines. But she had none of those things in this condo, and no idea where to get them, even if she dared leave Taylor and venture out in this blizzard.

She sat on the side of the bed and patted the Taylor-shaped lump under the blankets. "You have to take your medicine," she said. "And you can't do it on an empty stomach. If you have the toast and tea and take the pill that's for your stomach first, then after a bit you can take the other pills and your stomach will be able to handle them."

"No."

"Taylor, please. Do this for me."

Taylor's head emerged from the covers. "Where's Daddy?"

Darcy smoothed her hands over the blanket, determined not to betray her nervousness. "He's stuck at the hospital in Denver. It's snowing really hard and the roads are closed."

"I want my daddy." Taylor's face crumpled and she began to sob.

Darcy pulled her close, blinking back her own tears. She wanted Mike here, too. He'd know how to get Taylor to eat. He'd have medication to settle her stomach and lower her temperature. Darcy felt helpless.

How long could Taylor go without the antirejection drugs before her body rebelled against the heart she hadn't been born with? What were the signs of organ rejection? Darcy could call Mike and ask, but she hated to worry him further.

And she hated to hear more doubt in his voice. She was doubting herself enough for both of them. Was he thinking, as she was, that her best hadn't saved her own child?

She forced back the guilt and tears. This was no time for self-pity. She made her voice stern. "You're going to eat something and you're going to take your medicine," she said. "No more whining."

"I'm not whining." Taylor glared at her and sniffed.

"It sounds like whining to me."

"I want to talk to Daddy."

"After you eat and take your medicine, we'll call him." At least then she'd be able to report that much progress.

"You can't keep me from calling my own father."

"You can call him—after you eat."

"Why are you being so mean?"

"Obviously because I've been waiting to get you alone to pick on you. Now come on, sit up. Your toast is getting cold."

Taylor ate the toast and took the pills. Darcy felt a small surge of triumph. She felt even better when the girl didn't throw up again right away. Apparently exhausted from the effort of arguing and eating, Taylor fell asleep before Darcy could call Mike. Darcy breathed a sigh of relief and prayed the worst was over.

The phone rang and she answered it on the first ring. "How is she?" Mike asked without preamble.

"I got her to eat some toast and take her medicines," Darcy said. "She's sleeping now."

"I spoke with a doctor at the hospital there in Breckenridge. He said they can send an ambulance for her."

"An ambulance?" Darcy's heart pounded. "Is that really necessary?"

"It would be safest. They can administer antinausea drugs and IV fluids."

"Oh. If you think that would be best…"

"Let me talk to her."

Taylor was groggy, and slow to wake, but Darcy finally made her understand her father was on the phone. Darcy could hear Mike's voice clearly as he spoke to his daughter.

"How are you feeling, sweetheart?"

"Not so good. When are you coming back, Daddy?"

"I'll be there as soon as I can, but this storm has all the roads closed. I've got a doctor friend there in Breckenridge who's going to look after you though. He's sending an ambulance to take you to the hospital."

"No! I don't want to go to the hospital." Taylor's wail startled Darcy. The girl's cries drowned out Mike's reply.

"I want to stay here with Darcy. I don't want to go to the hospital with a bunch of people I don't know." Taylor began to sob again, and handed the telephone to Darcy.

"You've got to persuade her to go to the hospital," Mike said.

Darcy wanted Taylor in the hospital, where she'd receive expert care. But she was torn. She hated to see the girl so distressed. "She's really upset," Darcy said. "And she seems better now. She didn't throw up after she ate, and she doesn't feel as warm to me." She hadn't taken Taylor's temperature in a couple of hours, but she would as soon as she got off the phone.

"I'd feel better if she was with medical professionals," Mike said.

Darcy sighed. Of course she wasn't qualified to look after Taylor, but did Mike have to be so sure of it? "You're right," she said softly.

"Then persuade Taylor to go to the hospital."

Taylor sent Darcy a look, her big brown eyes brimming with tears. "I hate hospitals," she moaned. "Please don't make me go."

How sick was she if she could argue so forcefully against going to the hospital? Darcy hated hospitals herself, with their antiseptic smells and constant activity. She'd often thought they were among the worst places to try to get well. "What if Taylor stays here with me and I promise to call the ambulance if she gets any sicker?" she asked.

In the silence that followed, she wondered if Mike was grinding his teeth. "All right. But I'm going to call in some meds and arrange for them to be delivered, and if anything changes, you call me."

"Yes, sir."

He hung up without saying goodbye. Darcy gripped the phone, swallowing her hurt. Of course he was concerned about Taylor, but wasn't Darcy important to him at all? Did he have to be so brusque? She was doing the best she could, and it seemed to be working.

"Am I going to have to go to the hospital?" Taylor asked.

"No, honey. Not now, anyway." Darcy plumped the pillows behind Taylor's head and smoothed the sheets over her. "Your father is sending over some medication." Though how the delivery driver would get to her in this storm, she had no idea. "As long as you don't get any sicker, you can stay here with me, and your dad will join us as soon as he's able."

Taylor enveloped Darcy in a fierce hug. "I love you," the girl said. "I want you to stay with me forever."

"I love you, too." Darcy returned the hug.

She sat with Taylor until the girl drifted back to sleep, then moved into the living room, where she watched snow fall in a white curtain past the window, trying hard not to think about Mike and all the things she wished he'd said.

She must have nodded off. A knock on the door startled her. Groggy, she shuffled across the room to answer it and confronted what might have been a mini abominable snowman, but on closer inspection turned out to be a woman bundled in layers of down and polyester. "I'm Renee Jorgenson," the woman said as she stripped off gloves, goggles and hat and began unzipping a blue snowmobile suit. "I'm the nurse Dr. Carter hired to look after his daughter."

Darcy stared as Renee peeled off more layers, until the nurse stood before her in stocking feet, ninety pounds of skin and bones in a pink sweater and jeans. "How did you get here?" Darcy asked.

"Snowmobile. I stopped at the pharmacy on the way over and picked up the prescriptions Dr. Carter ordered." She lifted a backpack. "Where's my patient?"

"In her bedroom. She's sleeping now."

"I'll just take a look at her. Is it down this hall? No, you don't have to come with me. You must be exhausted. Why don't you get some sleep."

Darcy stared after her, relieved that a professional had arrived, and disappointed that she herself was so inadequate for the job. She sank to the sofa, the knowledge taking all the strength out of her legs. As much as she loved Taylor—and…Mike, too—Taylor's precarious health terrified her. The idea that Darcy might do something, even inadvertently, to endanger the girl was like an ax hanging over her relationship with Mike. Clearly he didn't trust her with his daughter. Maybe she wasn't qualified but she would never have done anything to endanger the girl. If Taylor had continued throwing up her medications or if her fever had risen Darcy would have been the first to call the hospital. Was it so wrong of her to wish the man had more faith in her than she had in herself?

MIKE SPENT a restless night in a hospital bed and woke early to reports that the roads were still closed. The snow had stopped, however, so he was hopeful the way would soon be clear for him to get to Taylor and Darcy.

A nurse brought him a disposable razor and a toothbrush and he managed to make himself presentable, then went in search of breakfast.

"Good morning, Dr. Carter. Did you spend the night here, too?" He looked up from pancakes and coffee into the round, weary face of Sarah Jankowski.

"Good morning," he said. "How is Brent this morning?"

"Better. Much better, I think." Her smile erased the worry lines from her face and banished the fatigue from her eyes. "I'm so glad you insisted on putting him in the hospital. I'd have been beside myself trying to look after him alone, in this storm."

"Where's your husband?" Mike recalled that Brent's father was some kind of skilled laborer, a plumber or an electrician.

"He's working on a new office building south of Denver and got caught when they closed the roads. He's spending a night with a friend."

"And your other children?"

"My sister lives two houses down, so they were able to walk over to stay with her."

Once again, her matter-of-fact handling of all these contingencies soothed him. "I'm glad to hear Brent is doing so much better," he said. "I'll stop by to see him in a bit." He wished Taylor was in the hospital, too, but his friend in Breckenridge had assured him Jorgenson was an excellent nurse.

After breakfast, he called the condo. "How is Taylor this morning?" he asked when Darcy answered.

"Much better, I think, but maybe you'd better let the nurse give you her professional opinion." Darcy's voice sounded distant, and the next thing he knew he was talking to the efficient Mrs. Jorgenson, who reported that Taylor's temperature was normal this morning and she was begging to be allowed to go out and play in the new snow.

Taylor took the phone next. "I'm okay, Dad." She sounded much more like an exasperated teenager than a ten-year-old girl should. "I don't know why you sent a nurse. Darcy and I were doing fine."

"I'll let Mrs. Jorgenson go home now," he said. "If you're really all right."

"I'm fine," she said. He could almost hear her roll her eyes.

"Good. I should be able to get there by this afternoon."

"I've missed you," Taylor said. "Drive careful. I love you."

He thanked Mrs. Jorgenson and told her she could go home, then asked to speak to Darcy, but was told she was outside shoveling the walkway. The condo association paid for people to handle that job, but there was no point explaining that to the nurse. "Tell her I should be there this afternoon," he said. "As soon as the roads open."

He hung up, a disquieting unease nagging at him. Was Darcy avoiding him? Or had he imagined her coldness? Surely she wasn't upset with him for leaving her alone with Taylor all weekend. Their romantic getaway hadn't turned out as planned, but he couldn't control the weather, and she'd said she understood about his patient. Melissa had said she understood too, at first, though later she'd grown to resent the intrusion of his medical practice on their lives.

He shook his head and went in search of his patient. No sense speculating on what awaited him in Breckenridge; he'd find out soon enough.

Brent was indeed better, literally bouncing on the bed when Mike walked in. "The steroids make him a little hyper," Sarah explained, with a fond look at her son.

"Did you see all the snow?" Brent asked. He pointed to the window, which was completely obscured by a wall of white. "I can't wait to get out there on my snowboard."

"Not for a few days yet," Mike said. He listened to the boy's chest, smiling at the clear breath and steady heartbeat. "But as soon as the roads open, you can go home."

"Thank you so much," Sarah said. "I don't know what we'd do without you."

The rewards of being a doctor were few enough,

but this was definitely one of them—the chance to be a hero to someone, at least for a while.

The roads opened an hour later and Mike joined the line of traffic streaming toward the mountains. He reached Breckenridge before noon and took the stairs to his condo, too anxious to wait for the elevator.

Taylor met him at the door, a long skirt pulled on over her flannel pajamas. "Darcy and I were dancing," she explained.

Darcy was dressed less flamboyantly, in jeans and an off-white sweater, her hair loose around her shoulders. "How are you?" he asked, moving forward to kiss her.

She turned her head, offering her cheek, not her mouth. Rebuffed, he stepped back. "Is something wrong?" he asked.

"Everything's fine," she said, but didn't meet his eyes.

Trying to hide his confusion, he turned to Taylor. "You're feeling better?" he asked.

"I'm fine." She rolled her eyes, hands on hips.

He took out his stethoscope. "Come here and let me listen."

She submitted to the examination, but moved away as soon as he let her. "It was just a stomach bug," she said. "I don't know why you had to make such a fuss."

He turned to Darcy again. She stood with arms

folded, her forehead creased in a frown. "You think I was overreacting, too, don't you?" he said.

"No, of course not," she said. "You wanted the best care for your daughter."

"I was a hundred miles away," he said defensively. "I had to make the best judgment I could."

"You did the right thing," she said. "I'm obviously not qualified to take care of a seriously ill child." She turned and left the room.

Mike looked at Taylor. But if he was hoping for sympathy, she offered none. "I think you hurt her feelings."

"I was only trying to take care of you," he said.

Taylor shrugged. "We would have been fine without the nurse."

He found Darcy in the guest bedroom, zipping up her suitcase. "What are you doing?" he asked.

"I think it's best I leave."

"I didn't mean to upset you," he said. "I thought you'd be relieved not to have the responsibility of looking after Taylor."

"Part of me was." She turned to face him, her eyes reflecting all the sadness he'd heard in her voice. "I was terrified I'd do something wrong. You obviously thought the same thing. I don't blame you. Really, I don't."

"Then why are you so upset?" he asked. "Taylor is not an ordinary child. Her situation—"

"I know all about her situation," Darcy said.

"That's my son's heart beating in her chest. I was ir-responsible enough to let him die, so how could you possibly trust me to look after her?"

He stared at her, the truth of her accusation freez-ing him. When she'd told him the story of her son's death, of how she'd left the boy with his father, an alcoholic, while she went to dance, he *had* thought her irresponsible. But no more irresponsible than he'd been in dismissing Taylor's first symptoms. He shared her guilt about the role he'd played in his child's suf-fering, but that didn't mean he didn't trust her. Did it? "I...of course I trust you," he finally stammered.

She shook her head. "I'm sorry, Mike. I wish things had worked out differently, but I...I can't take this. You don't trust me, and that makes me trust myself even less." She picked up the suitcase and pushed past him. He heard her saying goodbye to Taylor, then the door opened and shut quietly.

He didn't hear Taylor behind him so much as feel her presence. "Dad, why is Darcy mad at us?"

"Darcy isn't mad at us," he said. "She was just tired and needed to get home." He wanted that to be true, but the last look she'd given him told him he'd driven her away.

"I guess we should go home, too," she said doubt-fully. "I have school tomorrow."

Traffic was heavy, making the drive home even longer than usual. Taylor fell asleep in the backseat, leaving Mike to fill the silence with his thoughts.

What had he done that was so wrong? He'd only been trying to care for his daughter. Why couldn't Darcy understand that? He wasn't used to handing over her care over to anyone else. If her lapse in judgment about her son did affect his decision, it had been totally subconscious—and who could blame him for not wanting to take any chances with his daughter?

Maybe he had hurt her feelings, but she'd hurt him, too, being so quick to take offense. She must know how much she meant to him, after the night they'd spent together.

Hadn't he told her he loved her? They weren't words he uttered lightly, but saying them didn't mean he could change his way of thinking overnight.

Could he change, if it meant keeping Darcy in his life? Or did Taylor's illness, and his focus on taking care of her, coupled with Darcy's doubts about her own ability, ruin any hope they had of a successful relationship?

Melissa had once accused Mike of being too controlling to let her have a hand in taking care of her own daughter. At the time he'd denied the charge.

But today he wasn't so sure.

CHAPTER THIRTEEN

DARCY SHED more than a few tears over Mike the next few days. The fact that he didn't call to even try to persuade her to give him another shot proved her worst fears—that he agreed she couldn't be trusted with his daughter.

She tried to tell herself she was better off alone than taking on the responsibility for a child who was so fragile, but the thought brought no comfort. Until this weekend, she'd been much more comfortable around Taylor, less intimidated by the multiple medications and all Mike's warnings about germs and complications. She'd believed love and common sense, along with Mike's guidance and support, would be enough for them to handle whatever came along.

On Tuesday she was preparing for an evening class when a knock on the door interrupted her. "Carrie!" She ushered her brother's girlfriend—or former girlfriend—into the room. "It's so good to see you."

"It's good to see you, too. I stopped by to say goodbye."

"Goodbye?"

"I'm leaving town. Moving back to Michigan,

where my parents are. I'm going to work for my dad."
She folded and unfolded the ends of her scarf. "I'm
going to make a fresh start."

Darcy clutched the other woman's hand. "I'm so
sorry things didn't work out for you and Dave."

"Yeah, well, I still love him. But I'm tired of waiting for what's never going to happen." She lifted her
chin. "I want a husband, not a boyfriend. And I want
children and a house and the whole package. Dave
doesn't want that—or at least, he doesn't want it with
me."

"I'm sorry," Darcy repeated. "He's being stupid."

"I know there's someone out there for me," Carrie
said. "I can't say I didn't give Dave enough chances,
but I've waited long enough."

"What does he say?"

"That *I'm* being stupid." She made a face. "He
wasn't nice at all. He accused me of running home
to my mother because I couldn't get him to do what
I wanted. I told him a relationship took two people
and I was tired of being the only one who ever com-
promised. Things just got uglier from there."

"I wonder sometimes if men even think about how
they sound to us," Darcy said. By sending a nurse to
take over, Mike had sent a message loud and clear.

"I'm sorry," Carrie said. "How are *you* doing? Are
you still seeing that good-looking doctor?"

"It didn't work out between us."

"Rats. I was hoping you'd found someone. You deserve to be happy."

"We'll just have to work on being happy on our own," Darcy said. "I think maybe that has to happen before we can have a healthy relationship, anyway." She'd told herself she was happy before Taylor and Mike came into her life—or as happy as a woman who'd lost everything ever could be. But being with the two of them had only showed her how much she was missing.

"I need to remember that," Carrie said. "And I'd better get going. The movers are coming in the morning and I still have a lot to do. I only wanted to say goodbye. I'll miss you."

Darcy hugged her. "Keep in touch. You have my e-mail?"

Carrie nodded. "I will."

She left and Darcy tried but failed to focus on the transcribed deposition she was proofreading. She thought of Dave in his basement workshop, preferring to be alone rather than giving in one inch to what Carrie wanted. Was his life really so comfortable, or could a grown man really be so afraid of change?

Was *she* afraid of change? She'd told herself she was ready to be with someone—to be with Mike. But if that was true, why hadn't she fought harder for him?

She stood in front of the alcove by the door where the statue of Kali cradled the photograph of Pete and

Riley. When she'd placed the picture there it had comforted her to think of them together, protected. Their image in the alcove was both a reminder of the sweetness of their lives and the hole their absence left in hers.

She took the photograph from Kali's arms and stared down at Pete's roguish gleam and Riley's innocence. Then she carried the photograph across the room and tucked it in a drawer, along with other assorted photographs and papers. She didn't need this constant reminder anymore. She would always hold their spirits in her heart but now, finally, she was ready for more.

IF TAYLOR THOUGHT there was something amiss between her father and Darcy, she showed no sign of it when she arrived for class Wednesday. She greeted Darcy with a hug and immediately joined the others in discussing the upcoming show, which was to be held in the auditorium of the local high school. "Will there be a lot of people there?" she asked.

"Quite a few," Darcy said. "All my students, their friends and family."

"Is it a very big stage?" Zoe asked.

"It's a pretty big stage," Darcy said. "You'll have a chance to run through your number on it before the show so you can see what it's like."

"It's big," Hannah confirmed. "My brother Ben is in high school and we saw him in a play there."

"You'll be up where the audience can see you, but the lights make it difficult for you to see them," Darcy said. "Which is a good thing. It'll help you be less nervous. But because you'll be farther away from them, you want to be sure to wear stage makeup."

"Do you mean like a clown?" Debby asked.

"Not exactly," Darcy said. "But more blusher and lipstick and eye shadow than you'd ever wear in public. You'll see how the older dancers do their makeup and your moms can help you copy them. Now let's get started. We have a lot of work to do."

They spent the next hour drilling the routine, working on the fine details that took the dance from exercise to art. Darcy smiled at her young students in the mirror as she led them once more through the moves. They were so excited. Like any group of dancers, some were more talented than others, but all of them had gained flexibility and self-confidence these past weeks.

"Great job," she told them when class ended. "I'm very proud of how hard you've all worked. Remember, next week is dress rehearsal, so bring your costumes. And invite all your friends to come to the show in two weeks."

"Goodbye, Darcy!"

"See you next week!"

"See you tomorrow, Taylor!"

When the others had left, Taylor lingered behind.

"I guess your dad's running late again, huh?" Darcy said. Was Mike that reluctant to see her again?

"You said I should stay late again this week so we can finish my costume. Then you're going to take me home. Don't you remember?"

In everything that had happened this past week, Darcy had forgotten, but she didn't let on to Taylor. "Sure," she said. "Come on into the house and try it on."

"Oh my gosh!" Taylor squealed when Darcy pulled the completed costume out of the closet. "I love all the sequins you added. It's even more beautiful than I remember." She held it out to admire it, then threw her arms around Darcy. "Thank you so much. I love it so much. I love you for making it for me."

Darcy patted Taylor's back and swallowed a knot of tears. "You're welcome," she said. "I love you, too." For a long moment woman and girl embraced, Taylor's arms tight about Darcy's neck. As much as she regretted that things hadn't worked out with Mike, she mourned almost as much that she could never be more to this dear girl than a teacher and friend. What would she do when the class ended and she didn't see Taylor every week?

"I'd better go try it." Taylor pulled away, leaving Darcy bereft. "I can't wait to see what it looks like on."

Taylor skipped into the bathroom and returned

only moments later, walking on tiptoe with her arms outstretched. "How do I look?"

"Like a princess," Darcy said. "A beautiful princess. Now come stand on the chair so I can make sure the hem is straight."

Taylor obligingly mounted the chair. "Can you help me with my makeup at the show?" she asked. "I don't have any of my own." She made a face. "Dad says I'm too young for makeup and won't let me wear it."

"Your father's right, but this is a special case." Darcy adjusted the skirt. "I'll help you get fixed up. Don't worry."

"I came home from Mom's once wearing makeup and he got really angry."

"As I've told you, fathers sometimes have a hard time watching their little girls grow up," she said. Mothers too, but most hid it better, she thought. "We won't tell him beforehand and if he's upset later he can take it up with me." He already thought she was irresponsible when it came to his daughter, so a little makeup wasn't going to destroy her reputation.

She debated dropping Taylor off without speaking to Mike, but that was the coward's way out, so she followed Taylor up to the house, as if this was any other Wednesday afternoon, and not the Wednesday after he'd slept with her then left her with his sick daughter and run roughshod over her feelings.

"Come on in," Taylor said. "Dad has some awesome pictures of the storm." Mike was nowhere in sight when they entered the house.

While Taylor searched for the pictures on her dad's computer, Darcy nervously roamed the room. She'd thought she could get through this, could see Mike again and act like everything was fine, but there were too many reminders here of the man behind the doctor's white coat: pictures of a laughing, smiling Taylor on the swings in a park, a funny clay bird obviously crafted by a child's hand, Taylor's toys and school supplies scattered around the room.

His whole life revolved around his daughter. Why had Darcy imagined he'd ever have room in it for her?

She was hit by such overwhelming sadness she had trouble breathing. "Taylor, honey, I'm going now," she said. "I'll see you next week."

Before the girl could protest, Darcy slipped out the door. She was fumbling with the key when a familiar masculine voice called out, "Darcy, wait."

Mike wore a white dress shirt, and a purple paisley tie Darcy guessed was Taylor's choice. He was the picture of the handsome, eligible doctor, and her stomach did a backflip at the memory of him holding her in his arms.

"I'm glad I got to see you," he said, stopping a few feet from her car. His gaze searched her, as if looking for symptoms of some disease. "I wanted to say how sorry I was about the way things ended Sunday."

She nodded, blinking rapidly. She absolutely was not going to cry in front of him.

"I didn't mean to hurt you," he said.

She took a deep breath and forced herself to look at him—not at the handsome man she loved, but at the overprotective father who'd driven her nuts. "You were only doing what you thought was best for Taylor."

"And for you. I thought having the nurse there would make things better for you, too."

"I guess my…insecurity just proves I'm not ready yet to handle a relationship," she said. "Especially with a child involved."

"I guess I'm not, either. Maybe when Taylor's older…" His voice faded away.

"I'm glad she's okay," Darcy said.

"I'm not sure I can explain what it's like. Every illness is a flashback to that worst one, when I almost lost her."

"Maybe it will get better in time." Though could it, really? Did parents of chronically ill children ever regain the sense of ignorant imperviousness they'd known before their child was stricken? They knew a reality that was only abstract to everyone else—that the one thing you treasured most in this world could be snatched away from you in the blink of an eye. Was it any wonder Mike was determined to hold so tightly to Taylor? "I understand," she said. "I really do."

"I spent so many years raising her by myself—"

"You don't owe me an explanation."

She slipped into the driver's seat of her car and started the engine. "Goodbye, Mike. Take care."

She backed out of the parking space, glancing up only once to see him in the mirror, a solitary figure, hands in his pockets. She felt a heaviness in the pit of her stomach. Maybe that was the worst part of this— that a relationship once filled with hope and promise had ended, not with an explosion of emotion, but with a quiet slipping away. As if both of them had been so wrung out by grief and the weight of responsibility that they didn't have any fight left in them.

TAYLOR MET Mike at the door of the house. "Where did Darcy go?" she asked. "I was going to show her the pictures you took of the storm."

"She had to leave, honey." His hand at her back, he ushered her inside.

"Why was she in such a hurry?"

"She wasn't in a hurry. But she had to go." They'd both said all there was to say, so why prolong the pain?

Taylor sat on the sofa. "Dad, did the two of you have a fight or something?"

Her accusatory tone made him wince. "Not exactly a fight…. Look, honey, I know you like Darcy. I like her, too. But my job right now is to look after you and my patients. I don't really have time for anything else."

Taylor dismissed this reasoning with a shrug. "If she's mad at you about something, you should say you're sorry and promise to make things up to her. She'll understand."

"Oh, she will?" Taylor's certainty was almost amusing. "And what makes you such an expert?"

"I never said I was an expert. But I'm a girl." She tried to balance a pencil on one finger. "You should call her up and ask her out this weekend. Take her someplace romantic."

How pathetic was a man when his ten-year-old daughter started planning his dates for him? But Taylor definitely seemed to have everything worked out in her mind. "What are you going to do while I'm on this romantic date?" he asked.

"Well…" Her gaze was fixed on the pencil. "I could go to this party I've been invited to."

"What party is that?"

"It's a birthday party for this kid in my class."

Her evasiveness aroused his suspicions. "Does this kid have a name?"

Taylor blushed a deep pink. "It's Nathan Orosco."

"Na—isn't that the boy you gave a black eye? The one you punched for saying mean things to you?"

"Well, yeah."

Mike sat in the client chair across from her.

"Taylor, why would you want to go to a party given by a boy you dislike so much you fought with him on the playground?"

She dropped the pencil and looked at him at last, her eyes pleading. "I don't dislike him. I mean, I was mad about what he said, but I don't dislike him. And he said he was sorry."

"He said he was sorry," Mike repeated dully.

"Yeah. And Darcy and I talked about it. She explained about the way guys think, so his acting so stupid made sense—well, it made sense for a guy."

"Darcy explained… Then why don't you explain it to me so I can understand? You didn't like this boy, but now you do?"

"I didn't like him because I thought he didn't like me. But Darcy explained he probably really did like me and he was only trying to get my attention. She said guys do dumb things like that because they aren't always good at saying what they really feel."

Mike could concede that a fifth-grader might do something dumb like call a girl a name to get her attention, but grown men didn't act that way. *He* certainly didn't act that way. And as far as not being able to express his feelings, he'd told Darcy he loved her and he meant it—how much clearer could he be?

"Can I go to the party, Dad? Please?"

"When?"

"Saturday night, from seven to ten."

"At night?" Weren't kids' parties supposed to be in the daytime?

"Yes. His mom and dad are taking us to the ice-skating rink and for pizza."

Ice-skating sounded safe enough. As long as Taylor didn't fall and break something. "You promise me you'll be careful."

She rolled her eyes. "Of course I'll be careful. Please, Dad."

He sighed. What happened to slumber parties with girlfriends, or cake and ice cream with a clown in the afternoon? He supposed Taylor was getting too old for such things, though he hated to admit it. "I'll call and speak with Nathan's parents."

"Don't embarrass me by giving them a bunch of rules and telling them about my heart. Please."

"They need to know."

"They don't need to know. I'll tell them if anything important comes up, but you'll just freak them out. They'll tell Nathan and he'll look at me different. He'll think I'm some kind of weirdo."

"Taylor, having a heart transplant does not make you a weirdo."

"It makes me different. In fifth grade, that's enough."

She wanted so much to be like everyone else, but he could never see her that way—she was special simply because she was his daughter. But he wanted her to be happy as much as he wanted her to be safe. "I won't say anything. But I will call and introduce myself. That's only right."

She stood and came to hug him. "Thank you."

He held her longer than was absolutely necessary, reluctant to let her go. She was getting so independent, growing up so much faster than he wanted.

He'd known the day was coming, but he wasn't ready yet.

DAVE'S INVITATION to have dinner on Saturday caught Darcy by surprise. Of course, it was delivered in her brother's usual offhand manner. "I'm making ribs Saturday night if you don't have anything better to do."

She tried not to dwell on the fact that she didn't have other plans. Her brother was alone for the first time in five years. "I'd love to have dinner with you," she said. Maybe she could convince him to let go of his pride and ask Carrie back.

But the morose, heartbroken man she'd expected to find was nowhere to be seen. Dave greeted her with a bear hug and a kiss. "Come on back to the kitchen with me," he said. "I was just getting ready to baste the ribs."

The old-fashioned kitchen was clean but cluttered, the Formica countertop crowded with jars of spices and bottles of ketchup, molasses, vinegar and half a dozen other ingredients. "I'm experimenting with a new sauce," Dave said as he lifted the lid on a pot and stirred the contents. The sharp aroma of spices and vinegar made Darcy's eyes water.

"It smells wonderful," she said. She settled onto a stool at the end of the counter.

"I'm thinking of entering the barbecue competition the Lions Club sponsors in June," he said. He pulled a pan out of the oven and peeled back the foil to reveal a rack of smoky ribs.

"You'd get my vote," Darcy said. "When do we eat?"

"These need to cook another half hour or so." He began to baste the ribs, coating each one in sauce with all the meticulousness of a painter.

Darcy looked around the room. The red teakettle no longer sat at the back of the stove, waiting for Carrie to brew a pot of the tea she preferred over coffee. The puppy dog calendar had been replaced with muscle cars. The lace curtains she'd made were still at the windows. Had she left them to remind Dave of what he was missing?

"Have you heard from Carrie?" she asked.

"She posted on Facebook that she was settled into her new place."

"So you checked her page?"

"She's still on my friends list." He shoved the pan back in the oven. "Carrie and I don't hate each other," he said. "We're both better off now."

"How can you say that? You loved each other. You were together for five years."

"I loved her, but not the way she wanted. We were only together so long because I didn't want to hurt her. But I wasn't the man she needed—I didn't even want to be that guy."

"Didn't you want a home and family?"

He shook his head. "I'm happy with my life the way it is," he said. "Some of us are better off alone."

"I don't believe that." The idea was a weight pulling her down, and she fought against it.

"So how are things with you and Mike?" Dave asked.

She took a deep breath. "They didn't work out."

"No? I thought you were really into him."

"I was, but…" But what? The timing wasn't right, and they weren't ready. With Taylor in the picture, everything was too complicated. Since when had anything about love been simple? "It just didn't work out."

"I'm sorry to hear that. You okay?"

"Sure. I'm fine. Do you want me to set the table?"

"Yeah. I made potato salad, too."

She thought of the dinner Mike had made for her. What was it with all these independent men who could cook and keep house and live fine on their own and didn't really need women for anything?

She stood and began pulling silverware from the

drawer. Not that she wanted a helpless man—far from it. She only wished Mike had seen her as more capable. More worthy of his trust.

"You'll find someone," Dave said. "You seem ready now."

"What do you mean, ready?"

"Less sad, maybe? I'm not saying you don't still miss Riley and Pete—of course you do. But you don't seem as weighed down by the grief, as if there's room in your life now for more."

"You noticed all that?"

"Hey, I'm a man, but I'm not completely clueless." He pulled her to him in a rough hug. "Besides, I look out for my little sister. I want to see you happy."

"So you're okay alone, but I'm not?"

"I know how much having a family means to you. If this Mike guy wasn't right for you, you'll find someone who is."

"Maybe I should be on your barbecue cook-off team," she said.

"Are you serious?"

"Why not? It sounds like it would be a great way to meet guys who can cook."

He laughed. "You can be on my team if you promise to wear your belly dancing outfit."

"To cook barbecue?" She laughed.

"Absolutely. Most of the judges are men. You wear your costume and we'll be sure to pull in the most votes."

"I thought the barbecue was judged on how it tastes."

"Yeah, well, I've got that sewn up. But there's a showmanship trophy, too. We might as well go for that."

"Maybe I'll get a few friends to come. We'll call it belly-licious barbecue." She could picture their costumes—sort of a caveman theme, with leopard-print pants and wild fringe, maybe orange and red to resemble flames. Out of washable material, of course. She wouldn't want to risk anything fragile around all that barbecue sauce and beer. They'd dance to music with a strong drumbeat and a primitive sound. "I'll do it," she said. "You will win that showmanship trophy." She hugged him, hard. "Thank you."

"What are you thanking me for?" he asked, returning the hug.

"For reminding me of what I'm good at," she said.

"You mean dancing? You're the best."

"Not just dancing, but costuming and choreography and teaching." Maybe she wasn't an expert nurse or the world's best mother, but she had found her niche in the world. Dancing had gotten her through the worst time of her life, when she'd lost her husband and her son. It would get her through the loss of Mike and Taylor, too. And maybe, when Mike saw her dancing at her show he would realize that competence was sometimes overrated, and there was a definite place in the world for passion.

CHAPTER FOURTEEN

"COME ON, Dad! We're going to be late!" Taylor tugged on Mike's hand, towing him up the hill from the parking lot to the high school auditorium.

"We have plenty of time," Mike said. He leaned over to check his reflection in the side window of the car, and adjusted his tie.

"No one will be looking at you, Dad," Taylor said. "They'll all be watching the dancers."

"Of course." But there was one dancer he hoped might look at him. He straightened and studied Taylor, who was wrapped neck to ankles in her bathrobe. "Are you sure I can't have a quick peek at your costume?" he asked.

She folded her arms over her chest. "No. It's a surprise. Now come on!" Without waiting for him, she started across the parking lot.

Mike hurried after her. Others joined them in the trek up the hill: men and women and children and teens, some of the women swathed in capes and robes, the tiny bells on their costumes providing a soft soundtrack for their progress toward the auditorium.

Taylor turned to him once they were inside. "You find a seat," she said. "I have to meet Darcy and the others."

Then she was gone, leaving him standing in the doorway staring after her. When had his daughter become so grown-up?

A dancer brushed against him, a short dark-haired woman with purple feathers in her hair. She looked vaguely familiar. "Excuse me," she apologized, then hesitated. "Can I help you find something, Dr. Mike?"

She must be one of his patients. He searched his brain for the name. "No thank you—Mrs. Sheffield, isn't it?"

"Jane."

"Jane. I'm fine."

"Are you sure? You look lost."

He glanced around at the crowd of dancers and their friends and family and suddenly did feel lost, or at least out of his element. "I'm here with my daughter," he said, by way of explanation.

"Who is your daughter?"

"Taylor Carter."

The woman's smile broadened. "She's in the class with my daughter, Hannah. They're so excited about the show." She patted his arm. "You go on into the auditorium. I think there are still some seats up front."

"Thanks." He joined the line at the door and made

his way inside, accepting a program from a petite dynamo in turquoise veils.

"Enjoy our show," the woman said.

"Thank you." He had told himself he should enjoy it, but as the day had approached the heaviness in his stomach had increased. He kept thinking of the night he'd watched Darcy dance at the Middle Eastern restaurant. His emotions had been on a roller coaster ride ever since. He didn't plan on punching—or kissing—anyone tonight, but he'd stopped trying to predict how he'd act around Darcy. That last day at the Breckenridge condo he hadn't handled things well, and the few times they'd met since he'd hidden his true feelings behind a professional reserve.

Melissa had accused him of being emotionally distant, but not everyone was wired to bare his soul at the drop of a hat. Why couldn't Melissa—and Darcy, too—understand that?

He found a seat at the end of the third row with a good view of the stage and studied the program. Darcy opened the show. Taylor's group was third after that. Damn. He forgot his camera. Later, he'd have to try to get pictures from someone else. Melissa would want to see them, and he'd send one to his folks. Most of all, he wanted the photographs to help him remember this day.

"Excuse me, is someone sitting next to you?" A large woman with two children in tow stopped beside him.

"Oh, no." Mike stood to let them pass. He'd hoped Melissa would take time off to be here but she was somewhere in Europe. She'd sent flowers to the house and promised to join Taylor later in watching the video Darcy had hired someone to make, but Mike knew his daughter was disappointed.

The lights blinked and a regal woman with silver hair hanging past her waist moved to the center of the stage. "We're going to get started in a few minutes," she said. "I just have a few announcements." She read off a list of show sponsors and thanked some volunteers, then the lights dimmed and the music came up and the show began.

Mike recognized the pulsing rhythm and wail of strings and flutes he'd first heard at the Middle Eastern restaurant. Darcy glided onto the stage. She wore a costume of iridescent green and gold, multilayered skirts swirling to reveal tantalizing glimpses of her slender legs. A gold beaded belt encircled her hips and more gold outlined her breasts, which swelled above the V-neck of her costume. Her stomach was bare, and as she undulated, gold glitter reflected the lights.

Mike stared, scarcely breathing, transfixed by the grace and sensuality of her movements. Darcy danced with such confidence—such joy. She was so beautiful. So strong. She'd survived a great tragedy and rebuilt her life, yet he hadn't judged her strong enough to help him rebuild his.

He scarcely noticed the next groups of dancers. Why had he been so stupid, so afraid?

Then it was Taylor's turn. He leaned forward, holding his breath as the eight girls filed onstage.

His heart pounded. Where was Taylor? Had something happened to her? He half rose to rush backstage, then his gaze fixed on the girl in the middle of the front row—the one in purple and silver. Someone had piled her hair in ringlets and she was wearing makeup—elaborate eye shadow and liner and mascara, and glitter across her cheeks. She looked fifteen, not ten, but it was definitely Taylor, her smile broad, if a little nervous.

Mike sat back, all the breath knocked out of him. The music came up and the girls began to sway. He couldn't take his eyes off Taylor, off her costume. He'd thought at first her stomach and upper chest were bare, though mysteriously without scars. Then he realized she was wearing some kind of sheer body stocking. At first glance she looked just like the other girls.

Only more beautiful. And older. Watching her now was like looking through a lens into the future. Here was Taylor as a young woman, confident and happy, healthy and strong. Tears stung his eyes and he didn't bother to wipe them away. This was the dream he'd held on to all those tortured nights at the hospital while they fought to keep her heart going, waiting for a transplant, then hoping her body would accept the donor heart. He'd prayed for the chance to see Taylor grow up and tonight it was as if some genie had granted that wish.

No genie. He had Darcy to thank for this moment. Darcy, who had given his daughter her son's heart.

"Which one is yours?" the woman beside him leaned over and whispered.

"The one in the middle, in the purple."

"She's beautiful." She shoved a tissue into his hand. "I know just how you feel. Chokes me up every time I watch my sister dance."

The song ended and the girls took their bows to thunderous applause. Taylor grinned, then blew a saucy kiss over her shoulder as she exited the stage. Mike blotted tears, still stunned.

The feeling of numbness stayed with him through the rest of the show. Darcy danced again at the end, a lively, flirty number that brought the audience to their feet. Mike rose with them, applauding until his hands stung. "Isn't she amazing?" the woman beside him asked.

"Yes," he agreed. "Yes, she is."

He headed backstage as soon as the last notes of the last number died away. Taylor was engulfed in a crowd of well-wishers. Mike stopped in the shadows and watched her exchange hugs and congratulations with other dancers. What had happened to the self-conscious, lonely girl he'd lived with only a few months ago?

"Dad!" She stood on tiptoe and waved at him. "Did you see me?"

"You were beautiful." He hurried forward and hugged her tightly. "The prettiest dancer up there."

"Not the prettiest," she corrected. "That's Darcy. And some of the other women are really beautiful, too."

"And so are you." He smiled down at her. Up close the makeup looked a little garish. He felt a surge of relief as he recognized the girl behind all the paint. "You were gorgeous. Really. Your dance was wonderful."

"Thanks." She ducked her head and smoothed the spangles at her chest. "Do you like my costume?"

"It's terrific."

"Darcy thought of it. It's like the stuff ice-skaters wear. This way no one can see my scars."

"Did Darcy do your makeup, too?"

"Yes. You're not upset about that, are you?"

"It was a surprise when I first saw you, but I guess that's part of being onstage."

"It makes me look older, doesn't it?"

"Don't get any ideas about wearing it to school."

"Oh, Dad! I'd look ridiculous wearing all this gunk to school. But maybe some eye shadow...?"

"We'll talk about it later." He looked over her shoulder, at the milling crowd of dancers and friends. "Where's Darcy?"

"I think she's in her dressing room." Taylor took his hand. "Let's go find her."

They wove their way through the crowd, down a long corridor to a doorway. Taylor knocked. "Darcy, it's Taylor. Can I come in?"

"Sure, honey. It's open."

Taylor dragged Mike in after her.

Darcy, in jeans and a gauzy top, sat at a dressing table, peeling off a pair of false eyelashes. Her eyes widened when she saw Mike in the mirror and she turned to him, one spiderlike set of lashes still pinched between her thumb and forefinger. "Mike!"

"The show was wonderful," he said. *You're wonderful.*

"Thanks. I'm glad you liked it." She turned back to the mirror and began brushing her hair. Though most of the stage makeup was gone, she had glitter on her cheeks and around her eyes, as if she'd been sprinkled with fairy dust.

Mike suddenly felt awkward, a subject kept waiting before the queen. He guessed he couldn't blame her if she was cool toward him, considering how he'd frozen her out. Words filled his head, but he couldn't find the voice to say them.

Taylor came to his rescue. "Dad really liked my costume," she said.

"You were beautiful in it." Darcy's smile was all warmth again. "I'm so proud of you."

Taylor hugged the woman, eyes shining. Mike's

eyes burned and he fought back his emotions. "I'm proud of you, too," he said. He touched Taylor's shoulder. "Do you think you could leave Darcy and me alone for a bit?" he asked. "Don't wander off too far."

"Dad!"

"I know. You're not a little kid anymore. I know that. Even if I can't always accept it."

She kissed his cheek. "Kiss and make up," she whispered, then, giggling, scurried from the room.

"What did you want to say to me?" Darcy asked, still facing the mirror.

He wanted to tell her to turn around and look at him, but what right did he have to ask her for anything? "Watching Taylor dance, I realized how much you've done for her," he said. "She used to be so self-conscious about how she looked. So aware of all the ways being a transplant patient made her different."

"Taylor is a very special girl. What she's been through has made her older in some ways, yet she's managed to hang on to a lot of innocence."

"But you've brought out another side of her—you've given her so much confidence. We both owe you for that."

"You don't have to thank me. I love her as if she was my own daughter." Her eyes met his in the mirror.

"I didn't come here just to talk about Taylor." He took a step toward her and at last she did turn. "I'm sorry I acted the way I did that Sunday in Brecken-ridge," he said. "I was afraid."

"I was afraid, too."

"I wasn't just afraid for Taylor. I was afraid for me, afraid of giving up control. I think, with all that's happened these past few years—not just Taylor's ill-ness, but my divorce and my life being turned upside down—there was so much I couldn't control that I learned to keep a tight grip on everything else. From my schedule to my emotions. Especially my emotions. It was as if I convinced myself if I kept everything else in line, I wouldn't lose Taylor."

He began to pace, words pouring from him with each step. "Then I met you and that very first day I felt some of that control slip. You made me think things—feel things—I hadn't allowed myself to think or feel for years. It was unsettling. But I liked it. I thought I could handle it.

"That night at the condo was so incredible. When I left to return to Denver I was flying so high. Then Taylor got sick and it was as if I'd crashed into a wall. She needed me and I couldn't be there with her. Things were hurtling out of control and I had to stop it. So instead of letting you handle it, I did what I always do." He stopped in front of her. "That was wrong."

She pleated the hem of her top in her fingers. "I was scared, too," she said. "Afraid something would happen to Taylor. I made a wrong decision for Riley and it cost him his life. What if I made the wrong decision for Taylor?" Her eyes met his. "I was angry you didn't trust me, but part of me thought maybe you were right. Since Riley and Pete died, I've avoided responsibility—I don't even have a dog. I told myself I was being smart, giving myself time to heal.

"Then I took a chance with you and Taylor and when that didn't work out I thought it proved I didn't deserve to be happy."

"You do deserve to be happy." He squeezed her shoulder. "And I deserve a life where I don't always have to be responsible for everything. I'm learning to let go of some things, but I don't want to let go of you."

He pulled her up beside him and kissed her, a long, drugging caress that said more than words ever could. When at last their lips parted, she pressed her face into his neck, her arms wrapped tightly around him. "Will you give me another chance?" he asked.

"Yes. I'll give *us* another chance." She kissed his neck, then his cheek. "I love you, Mike. I couldn't say it that night at the condo, but I'll say it now."

"I love you, Darcy. I want us to be together—you, me, and Taylor."

"I want that, too. More than anything."

"WHAT'S GOING ON in there?" Hannah nudged Taylor's shoulder. "What do you see?"

"They're kissing." Taylor eased the door open an

inch wider so she could get a better view. Her dad looked happier than he had in days.

"That's good," Hannah said. "Right?"

"It's good." Taylor eased the door shut again and let out a sigh. "Now if I can just keep Dad from doing any more stupid guy things."

"Duh! They can't help it. I think it's genetic."

"And I guess women aren't always perfect, either."

"Close to it. Hey, speaking of stupid guy things, what did Nathan say to you at his party last week? I saw the two of you sneak off to that alcove by the soda machines."

Taylor hoped all the makeup she was wearing hid her blush. "He just wanted to apologize again for saying those mean things about me the day I hit him."

Hannah smirked. "I think he wanted to get you alone so he could kiss you. Did he?"

"Did he what?" Taylor pretended not to understand.

"Did he *kiss* you?"

"Maybe." It was only a little kiss. His lips tasted like root beer.

She turned back to the dressing room and eased the door open once more. "They're still kissing."

"I think Darcy would be a cool stepmom," Hannah said.

"Yeah." Taylor closed her eyes and made a

wish—for her dad and Darcy to love each other forever, and for the three of them to be a family. What she'd wanted all along, with all her heart.

* * * * *